Chapter 1

He stood out of the way of the other commuters as they corralled themselves into a queue, leaning against the side of the tunnel entrance, struggling to finish the last bite of his footlong without dripping the deluxe fixings on his clothes. It reminded him of the lineup for Dante's Inferno, the ride at a strange little family-run carnival he used to go to as a kid, that would pop up out of nowhere, unannounced, on the fringes of the city. Sometimes shifty looking ride attendants that he'd recognized from the creaky Mouse Trap roller coaster, or the wobbly Gravitron ride would double down, slipping on masks of generic spooks and demons and hide around paper mache corners, jumping out just as the coal-car rounded a bend in the track. The tunnel promised a genuine glimpse of hell itself for a shekel.

He'd tried again to resist the temptation to skip this part of his daily ritual to no avail. It was virtually impossible to walk by the cart, get a whiff of the slowly rotating weiners on the fat soaked spit, burnt onions, and the other essentials—mustard and relish having a scent powerful enough to cut through the snow, rain, heat, gloom of night, and his resolve, without ponying up for one of those locally famous hot dogs.

He spent over seven hundred dollars a year on them and knew the vendor by name, or so he thought. This sum he'd calculated on his recently upgraded phone, on one of those rare rides he had enough elbow room to use the app. The vendor loathed when regulars tried to be overly familiar with him and used trite handles like *Buddy*, or the even more cringe-worthy *Bro*, during what to him was meant to be and always had been for time immemorial, silent transactions.

Sucking the last glob of mustard from his thumb, he descended against the warm, noxious breath of the tunnel that whooshed from the depths with the arrival of a train, and down infinite sets of steps leading to the dais. He ignored the flashy ads for perfumes and cell phones with random names like *Shoop, Kokorico,* and *Huawei,* and the models with faces like flawless diamonds; cut into impossible angles, a cubist's interpretation of the human face. They were meant to entice the consumer into pawning their current cell back to the provider at a significant loss, necessitating the purchase of another; the latest-greatest upgrade of your perfectly fine, but now only newish phone. The 6.5 rather than the 6.0. As if that half millimeter increase in diameter represented a quantum leap in telecommunications technology.

He preferred the old-manly scent of Brut, which came as a part of a box set that his wife bought for him every Christmas, as evidenced by the vast collection of slimy soap on a rope, dangling from his shower head. Besides, by the time everyone had gotten around to sliding their Christmas cracker crowns on their fat heads, his rich twat cousin's expensive, behind the showcase, Eau de cologne, pretty much smelled the same as his middle of the road aftershave: usually stocked beside the cotton swabs and rubbing alcohol.

He also wondered why they couldn't get average joes like himself as spokesmodels, thinking he made off the rack couture look pretty damn-good, or so his wife would say, but only after a tipple of the ripple, one of the big-box jobbies that could double as vinegar for fish and chips. He saw the retro-rebel with a greaser's ducktail smoking a cigarette (indoors of all places), reading a hotrod mag, and wondered if it was safe to pull out his old flip phone from the junk drawer to bring to work.

Would his co-workers think of him as being hip and retro, too? He'd already begun to insert old gangsterisme from noir films that he was obsessed with from the time he was a lonely and impressionable little kid. He'd drop them in casual conversations with varying effect—mostly awkward, to distinguish himself from his homogenous colleagues. They'd get it eventually, but many a espresso machine chat would die in the meantime. 'Hey, fella,' he'd say, when he saw the rockabilly, hoping for an acknowledgement one day, to get some tips on implementing changes in his own life to assert his individuality. For now he counted on osmosis.

He loved the clicking sound of his heels on the tiles because it meant he was a hop, skip, and a jump from home. Once, after work, and having knocked-back a couple of beers and another one of those glorious tube steaks, he'd even managed to come out of himself long enough to perform a sort of—Gene Kelly, skip down the last steps and onto the platform, finishing his impromptu routine with a half-hearted flourish of jazz hands. Not today, however. Today was Friday; the Sunday of commuting, and a day of atonement for lapsed commuters. He'd be lucky if he didn't miss three trains before cramming himself aboard one of the overflowing carriages, and twist himself like a contortionist to face the window, so as not to breathe in other people's stale air. His shallow exhalations, a futile attempt to maintain a respectful telephone booth's worth of distance between himself and the other working stiffs.

He inched his way into the amorphous crowd and swayed with them as they attempted to gain ground toward hopefully, catching the second or third train with him. This part of his daily grind usually induced anxiety leading to a migraine, but today was different. His inner-voice was eerily calm and soothing sounding, like Karen Carpenter singing *Close To You* whispering softly, almost sweetly, 'It'll be okay, just get it over with.'

Amongst them was a demon. The bogey was leaning against one of the perfume posters: a thing of supreme ugliness blotting out depictions of contemporaneous beauty. You could only see it if you were one of the gifted, goofy, or dying from some wasting disease; so today it walked freely, unfettered by the annoyance of the astonishment of those pesky clairvoyant types. Its slimy gray head was curtained by long, curly black hair, and even blacker, opal eyes. They were fathomless, and one could only discern what it was gawking at by the direction the things head turned. This action performed with spasmodic, bird-like herky-jerks of its elongated neck. That is if you could see him.

This thing was christened Taob by Abramelin but preferred the handle, Gaap, as it was easier for wannabe witches, warlocks, stoners, and himself to pronounce. Gaap was the name he answered to when summoned. Besides the transit authority had been kind enough to paint his office shingle on the safety stripe of the platforms, though had misspelled his name. Mind The...

Gaap grinned, as with a crack of his neck, he spotted the man he was after. It was the one who'd narrowly averted getting mustard on the garish tie his wife had given him the previous Christmas and also came with deluxe Brut gift sets. Gaap's teeth were piranha-like and reeked of stale nothingness, as he'd not eaten a thing but souls for centuries. He delighted in this odiferous power of his by burping and blowing in the faces of his unsuspecting passersby.

He continued to surveil his subject while fighting against his tendency when concentrating to bob his head like a chicken, and finally spied the man as he squirmed his way to the front of the crowd, and closer to the precipice of the platform.

Humans always feel like the rush of wind through my belly, he thought, as he passed right through the throng, and took a position directly behind his subject. Gaap tutted as he gave him the old once-over. Another schlub, he thought, looking at the mark's rumpled, day-old, middling-level suit. He knew him by name, Tom it was, having added it to the murmurs of eternity after having taken too many a man before their time on errands past.

Tom sniffed at the air as if catching a whiff of something rank coming from behind him. It smelled like his seventh-grade geography teacher's breath, the unfortunate result of a steady diet of coffee and sneaky cigarettes in the out of bounds area of the schoolyard. He shrugged it off and tapped an envelope against his thigh. Gaap raised his hands and placed them an inch or two from Tom's back because to make actual contact would send a shiver down the intendeds spine, and alert them to the presence of something other.

The familiar sound of rolling thunder, screeching metal, and the spillage of light on to the track brought a smile to his face as he was one step away from being conveyed safely home. Gaap made a pushing motion, compelling Tom's feet past the safety stripe. He tried to shake off whoever was crazy enough to play such a sick joke and pushed back but met with an immovable force. He clenched his teeth, made an incorrect fist (as his karate teacher always pointed out) and spun around to punch the bastard capable of this—a potentially lethal prank. Gaap grinned goofily, clowning around with the other commuters as if they could see him and made a shoo motion with his splayed hands. Then lastly, with a cheeky flick of his long, bony finger, propelled Tom, who flapped his arms like a sickly birdy, attempting to regain its foothold—smack into the conductor's compartment; rag-dolling his body on to the electrified rails.

Sounds competed for supremacy: the ear-piercing screech of forged driving wheels clashing with the emergency brakes, shrieks from the bellows of horror-stricken faces, the crack and crunch of back and bone, and the sickening squish of gelatinous innards popping forth. Then, just as if God had suddenly jerked out the plug of a stereo blasting the crescendo of The Beatles *A Day In The Life,* the maelstrom-stopped dead.

Intermingled with the mortuary-like silence and gentle burbling of the tunnel stream you could almost hear Tom's last waking thought: Jesus, I smell like the days-end crap on my old Mcdonald's kitchen floor and his last memory—the promotion from the bun station to the manager of the whole shebang and the perk with the dollar an hour pay raise of having to weigh the garbage before putting it in the dumpster.

Gaap passed through the closed doors of the car and waved bye-bye to the pandemonium that had just as quickly resumed under the proscenium. He sallied into the conductor's compartment and with mild curiosity watched as the driver clutched at his heart. His head had blown up like a big red balloon, and teeny capillaries made num-num noises as they exploded from under his clammy skin. He looked to Gaap, help me, pleading from his bulging eyes.

He can see me, Gaap thought. It meant that he was close to death. Gaap could do him a solid and put an instant end to his miserable life of quiet desperation (he thought that was how the saying went), but no one had ever paid him any such kindness. 'Nope, sorry pal, but you'll just have to suffer as I did.'

He flicked him in the nose as was his wont when dealing with flies and humans, then knelt and plunged his arm through the compartment floor, retrieving the envelope from the slimy pile of offal. The driver made one last desperate gasp for air before succumbing to his fated coronary, slumping over, and easing into the final death rattle.

Gaap leaped from the blinking console and landed with a crunch of his army boots on the gravel that lined the tunnel. He whistled something atonal as he toddled toward the gloom. It was vaguely familiar, which was the rub of this particular realm. The thing he bitched about most with his fellow minions. Everything was vaguely familiar and ghost-like, just like the poor schmuck who'd jumped in front of the train.

As his silhouette was about to be subsumed by the darksome he made a sudden left, just in case he was being shadowed and disappeared into the wall.

Chapter 2

Tom was on a train now. A car jammed with...people? There were no seats. It was standing room only, like a cattle car or the festival seating at a concert. All of them clamored for an eyeballs worth of window, clawing at the fogged glass like lizards trying to scale an aquarium. He was dying for a look-see himself, but when he even intimated his intention, another one of the creatures would spin around and confront him; nose to protuberance. They had faces like an Edvard Munch depiction of human suffering, and whispery remonstrations if he were to be so bold as to even hint at taking another's spot. So he, perhaps wisely, demurred. What the hell?

And so again, and again. The question ricocheted from temple to temple until it burst forth from Tom's mouth in the form of a life-affirming scream. He looked around to see if there were any reactions to this tick, but they were all too busy screaming themselves to pay him any mind. Speaking of him, who was he? Where? How did he get there, and where was he headed?

The train screeched to a halt, sending a pack of them careening down the aisle, and leaving a sudden opening for him to fly out the sliding doors. He bolted, thinking he'd be followed by at least a few of his fellow passengers, who might wisely avail themselves of the same opportunity to escape, but they slid slowly shut, leaving only him and inky black, cat-sized scavengers, skulking amongst windswept trash on the platform and bickering over a docked cigarette butt.
Am I in hell, and if I am—why?

He got to his feet and oddly, stood at attention as they pulled out of the station, sensing perhaps that he'd escaped a fate even worse than his current predicament, once the route terminated.

He kicked at the vermin and walked over to the wrought iron railing, looking down to the cracked, rain-slick street below. He had seen this type of raised subway platform before, but only in movies about the mean streets of New York.
Tom wondered, is that where I am?

If so, he knew from his favorites like *Taxi Driver* that there'd be more than mutant rats with which to contend.

He peered up at the sky and watched as a giant bird-like creature, swooped down and picked off something running for cover down a noirish-looking alleyway. Its prey protested in shrunken human tones as they achieved lift-off past fire escapes slung like art deco jewelry off the sides of the buildings.

That wasn't a rat or carrion in its talons; it was a little person. A cryptographer..., no, cryptozoologist, would have a field day trying to categorize this Animalia Domesticus. He wondered now where he stood in the food chain and looked around for something to defend himself. Christ knows, there were probably other yet to be discovered or once thought extinct monsters to go along with the mythical birds of prey.

Okay, Tom thought, he knew he was a 'Eugene' because nobody he knew used that kind of nerdy reference or terminology when thinking to themselves or aloud while making observations, and wisely avoided them in casual conversation. So he was not cool here either. Sparking off his vocabulary, he naturally wondered what he looked like but didn't hold out much hope for his prospects with the ladies. He hacked a loogie and waited forever for it to splatter on the pavement. It was a long way up. For a second, he thought about climbing atop the railing and leaping off into the great black yonder; as this had to be a dream. One of the archetypal ones, mind you—the kind he had as a kid when stressors at home or school invaded dreams to ventilate. However, even in his dreams, he'd come crashing down to earth only to be swarmed by his tormentors and ripped to shreds. Nope, it was a long way down.

He gripped the cold railing, tickling rust, and raindrops upon the street as he clanged down the perforated steps to the warped pavement below. The reflection of a fifties-style diner undulated gently amongst oil-slick rainbows in a puddle that ran the length of the road. He stepped off, breaking up the romantic, Rockwellian rendering into wavelets, waiting for it to reconstitute around his feet, but it had vanished into the shallows. Confused, he looked up. The only buildings in the area were either boarded-up warehouses with saggy loading docks and flaky hand-painted signage or derelict storefronts with soaped up windows. He felt a gentle breeze or was it something's breath, rustling the hair on the back of his neck. The whole thing was one great big pile of desolation and loneliness, and the wind whistled a hollow note. Tom felt helpless and overwhelmed like the time he got separated from his mom in a colossus shopping mall while she rushed to finish her Christmas shopping and left him to be snatched up by the man with teacher's breath and sticky hands. He was a pretty little kid back in the day as they all are for a while.

He heard the sharp, staccato rhythm of stiletto heels and the swish of an A-line skirt in perfect time to a backbeat rhythm that echoed up the alleyway and followed their amalgamated music. Hopefully, she too was a nighthawk in search of the diner.

The whiskey-scorched growl—evil sounding voodoo thing, of Howlin' Wolf, moaning *Smokestack Lightning*, boomed and rattled from a juke joint in the distance as he emerged from the depths of the alleyway. He half-expected to be confronted by a few more nostalgic, cinematic flourishes and wasn't disappointed. There was pleasant steam pouring forth from the sewer grates, and bums gathered around an oil drum fire, passing a bottle while singing an acapella ode to sleeping rough. However, where was the stench of piss and real filth? He wondered. There was something too clean about the atmospherics like they were props for an abandoned movie.

If not, the urban planner should've gone all the way with the renewal and inevitable gentrification of this skid row with a few strategically placed retro—urban items. Maybe a coat of fire engine red on the distressed hydrants and some old-fashioned telephone booths outfitted with the latest in video telephony technology? To top off the retrofit, a newsstand with a corner boy in a snap cap, flogging a stack of Wired magazines. He saw now that this stretch of the street already had the whole vintage neon sign thing going for it.

He caught one last glimpse of the woman before the door to the diner was chivalrously opened for her by a bundled-up man heading out to brave the sad, desolate streets of this lonesome town. That's the ticket, he thought, snapping his fingers and what he decided to call it. He could hear the haunting Ricky Nelson ballad as the dame (he was itching to insert the colloquialism into a conversation—feminism be damned), froze for an eternal moment before breezing in. As if to show off the black racing stripes that ran up the length of her white silk stockings and strode inside, taking a window booth with a perfect view of the street, then cat-like, fixed her sights on something—him.

They played chicken with their eyes. Tom gave way first, breaking eye contact just before the butterflies became the ache. Again, he wrestled with that vaguely familiar feeling of the place. The diner had a picture-postcard quality that Tom had seen and admired somewhere before, maddeningly on the cusp of being a full-blown deja vu without the halcyon reverie when one feels transported through time.

Suddenly, The warm pool of blood-red light in which he was standing began to flicker like the back-wall projection of the home movie he used to watch by himself in the basement. The disintegrating memento of his phantom father waving frantically from the past. He looked up to see the tubing of the neon diner sign, snakily reform into the unmistakable, sweeping penmanship of his late father; the blinking salutation: Dear Tom.

At once he was thrust back to the rumpus room of his childhood home, running a pudgy little finger along the splotchy cursive on a bent picture-postcard. His head buzzed as he skipped to the parting words, that even in this dream within a dream state felt merely perfunctory: Love Dad. A mournful howl, the flutter of wings, and the stealthy patter of paws coming from somewhere behind him confirmed his suspicions that this alternate reality was full of heretofore unknown forms of danger and bade him inside.

A brass bell rang as he entered. The dame was sitting in a corner window banquette, ignoring his presence with a studied diffidence, took a long, mean draw from an unfiltered cigarette, but ruined the effect that would have been really sexy, if she didn't clinch it between her teeth, and withdraw it from pasty lips with her thumb and forefinger in the unladylike fashion of a common gun moll. She blew thick plumes of smoke from her mouth and allowed the remainder to waft lazily from her nostrils, obscuring her face in a cumulus smog.

The joint was jumping as Fats Waller would say. The blues music throbbed from a gaudy Wurlitzer jukebox, and everything glowed with an aura of eerie, lime-green light, that seemed to him to be sourceless, but yet, was everywhere. The pageantry, posturing, and multidimensional costumes of the other customers gave

Tom the impression that he was the lone intruder at someone's campy party. However, there was one man who stood out from the rest. He was wearing a bowler hat, lived-in Victorian-era suit, and a thick gold watch fob drooped conspicuously from his breast pocket. The gentleman was sitting at the end of the lunch counter, perched atop a stool, puffing contentedly away at a spindly pipe, rather than everyone else's seemingly mandatory choice of cigarettes, and penciling over the already completed crossword in a newspaper dated: *April 11th, 1954.*

Tom sidled up beside him and watched as the man, who despite the wadded up napkins protruding from his ears, whinged to the beat.

'Infernal racket,' he spat, aiming his contempt at the whirling jukebox, and a formally dressed couple tucked beside it, affecting a listless, zombie-like box step. He noticed Tom eyeballing him and turned his residual disdain toward him.

'Oh, sorry,' Tom said. 'It's just, I know this is a dream, and hopefully, I'll wake up before I miss my stop. Happens all the time.'

The man seemed genuinely saddened by Tom's

explanation.

'You're new here aren't you, you poor, poor, thing,' he said, shaking his head.

'This isn't a dream?' Tom said incredulously, with a twist of scepticism.

The man put down his paper on the marbled Formica countertop and inhaled deeply as if about to recite the monologue from a long-running play for the millionth time.

'Of a sort, I suppose. Allow me to introduce myself, Aleister Crowley.' The man extended his translucent hand, offering it to shake or kiss, he wasn't sure.

'Tom, I think, from the sign.'

'Welcome to April eleventh, nineteen fifty-four, Tom. The most uneventful day in recorded human history.'

Tom pulled back sharply as if burned by ice. Aleister continued: 'Do you recognize this place?'

Tom looked around again and conceded that he did indeed, his inner voice responding in a posh English accent influenced by Aleister's. 'Sort of, reminds me of a postcard my Dad sent me from the road once.'

'Postcards, posters, prophylactics, by now, no doubt. The bloody thing's become as much of an American institution as apple pie. Simply baffles me that the banal rendering of a quaint scene from an American greasy spoon could inspire such reverence and ravings from experts, laymen, and lunatics alike. You, my friend, are a permanent patron of Edward Hopper's prototype for tourist trap trinketry: *Nighthawks*.

'Oh yeah, the calendar,' Tom said.

'That too,' Aleister said, ruefully. 'Bastards never gave any of my paintings—mostly self-portraits, the recognition they deserved or my voluminous writings for that matter.'

'You're an artist,' Tom said, his curiosity piqued.

'A renaissance man, you might say,' he said with prideful gravitas. 'I take it that Crowleyania has yet to usurp Christianity?'

'Wait a second,' Tom beamed, finally recognizing the bald head and angry cherubic face of the man sitting before but not able to put a name to it. 'You're that guy...on, on, the cover of *Sergeant Pepper's*.'

'Yes.' Aleister sighed, dejectedly. 'The one and only.'

'Cool. I wish I had my copy. I'd get you to autograph it.'

'Yes, you'd be the type. Now, take a look around the

cafe. My Father used to say that you could judge a place's level of cleanliness by checking behind the commode.'

Tom made to get up to check for himself but was dissuaded by Aleister's paternal hand on his shoulder.

'Just observe your immediate surroundings more closely.'

Through the haze of cigarette smoke and a tendency to be blinded by his nostalgia for all things pre-1973, noticed a forked crack in the shape of a lightning bolt, running the length of the back wall to the raven-black bouffant of the woman in the booth. And that the bright, canary-yellow paint was the staining from decades of trapped fag fumes. The tin ceiling panels bulged and bursting like infected pustules weeping droplets of grey matter on to the tables of oblivious patrons below. Lastly, he picked at the curled corner of the checkerboard floor. It was loose and shifty. Dry scabs not quite ready to be yanked from still healing wounds.

Tom was incredulous. 'What's causing all this damage?' Aleister continued:

'You've heard of those savage tribes refusing to have their pictures taken for fear that it would steal their souls?

'Yeah, on National Geographic,' Tom said. 'Made the bra look more important than the wheel until implants came along.'

'Well, that same phenomena is happening with *Nighthawks*. With each reproduction of Hopper's painting, another layer of patina is wiped from the original, thus exposing it to the elements. This building is condemned, Tom, and if we're evicted, we'll be jettisoned to one of the other, less interesting realms, and it's not on angel's wings we'll be conveyed. Our seedy little sanctuary will cease to exist. This limbo dimension—if that's what it is—is the only buffer between heaven and hell. Please tell me you were sent here by the more compassionate—New Testament version of God.'

'Phew, Tom said, wiping the imaginary sweat from his brow. 'You better check your pipe, Mr. Crowley. Cause that sounds like the synopsis for an episode of the Outer Limits. Sent here. Like who, Jesus Christ— Terminator? He was squeezing his nut sack between his thighs in a failing bid to wake up. Then he remembered a stupid, inconsequential moment from his past. 'I gave that stuff up back in high school after a bad trip. Thought I was impervious to pain so I put my hand in the blender but couldn't figure out how to turn it on.'

Aleister looked defeated and reflective. 'Breezed through the pearly gates, but the bastards busted me while boarding the astral train,' he said, returning to his paper.

'I need a drink,' Tom said, muttering like the bemused and inconsolable victim of a hit and run.

Chapter 3

A swampy mug of coffee appeared before Tom. He greeted it with the enthusiasm of a pedestrian whose just stepped in dog shit.

'I mean, something that tastes like airplane glue smells.'
Aleister shook his head with the solemnity of a priest about to read Tom his last rites.

'I'm afraid the only beverage served here is that cack they call coffee, and as for vittles—this soggy confection they have the cheek to call apple pie.' He pointed to a stone-cold mess of the stuff, unceremoniously slapped on the counter. 'I suggest you have it buried a la mode.'

'Fag?'

'Nope, never,' Tom said on both accounts.

Aleister slid him a pack of 'Unlucky' cigarettes anyway.

'If you're looking for an eye-opener or two, we'll have to head over to a little speakeasy I know all too well. A friend of mine runs it. Civilized for a Chinaman. Goes by the name, Fu.'

With the mention of Fu and his booze can, as if she was reading their lips, the lady in the booth jumped up, quickly smoothed down the wrinkles in her dress, slapped another coat of lipstick on her swollen, ruby red lips, and checked her ghostly reflection in the sweaty window. She sidled over to them and wedged her buxomness between a vacant barstool and Tom. She smiled sweetly and stiffly to reveal the cracked and stained veneers of her crooked teeth. He stifled a grimace, patted his pockets and shrugged, to say—I'm skint. She harrumphed and spun around to encroach on Aleister's space, nearly stabbing his eye out with her protruding ciggie.

'Got a light?'

Tom scrutinized the damage. She was in the same

dilapidated state as the dinette but her luster was rubbed raw. She reminded him of one of those ancient queens who'd forgo a bath for another layer of spackle and perfume, and was deathly still, avoiding any sudden movements so the facade of her face wouldn't crumble away to reveal a *Dorian Gray* type monster, glowering under the surface. Again with that fucking, vaguely familiar feeling.

Aleister dutifully lit her smoke, and she inhaled greedily; her lungs sounding asthmatic; wheezy on the bottom with ropey mucus on top. Tom heard that sound recently, he thought. It was a death rattle.

She smiled at Tom. A big, dumb, moldering grin. She teased the wings of her dusty coiffure and cocked her head like a used up Mae Clark to his James Cagney. A coquettish automaton with a broken neck. 'Ain't you gonna introduce me, Al?' He wished he had the guts to stuff something in her face.

'Oh, yes, forgive me.' Tom, meet the Black—

'You probably don't need to cause' I'm real' famous!'

'Dhalia,' Aleister sighed.

Tom thought that to chew gum and smoke at the same time was cheap and loathsome.

'Recognise me?' She struck a pose.

'Yeah, Tom said, pondering the wreck of a woman that stood before him. 'From autopsy photos and those...true crime documentaries.'

Aleister cringed and slumped over his paper, pretending to busy himself with the now shredded crossword.

'If you're good I'll show you my scars.'

Tom thought back to the monochromatic, black and white crime scene photos he'd seen of her chopped-up remains, probably in a book he'd flipped through on a toilet somewhere. He remembered the vision of her splayed, beluga white-body with the torso and limbs lying akimbo in the tall grass. The clean, bloodless cuts of flesh with ends like cartoon hams. However, mostly, that wicked grin carved into her cherubic face. She was a perfect mix of the vixen and innocent waif, in life, if not in death. It wasn't a crime of frenzied passion but a bloodless, methodically executed-bordering-on-surgical-dissection, then ceremoniously displayed, rather than concealed in a vacant lot for the whole world to see. The exhibit seemed to rage forth: THIS IS WHAT HAPPENS TO WHORES WHO FUCK WITH ME!

He wondered why some corn pone hick—wannabe starlet from the midwest, who undoubtedly turned the occasional trick to make ends meet ended up here. Wasn't she an innocent victim of the Hollywood meat grinder and a naive John—turned delusional, murderous sugar daddy?

That's how he remembered it. However, only vaguely.

Now Tom wondered if ever he'd be able to scavenge enough scraps of memory to place in a coherent sequence, then tape them together to create a mental montage of his past. Just like he'd painstakingly accomplished with the little bits of Super 8 film he'd found of his father in a box under the stairs. There it goes again, he thought. Would there be memory enough to ascertain the why of his present circumstances? He didn't even have the means to conjure up a mental image of what he looked like, let alone a full-blown recollection. Only involuntary flashes of objects and insignificant incidences, like the hastily scrawled note from his dad on the back of the picture-postcard, the warbly reflection of this Tom guy in the mud at the bottom his coffee cup, and a yearning for the movie of his life to commence.

Tom began to notice other noteworthy personalities and genuine-article celebrities milling around. He saw Bobby Kennedy and Marilyn Monroe come out of the can, still trying to maintain the pretense of a purely platonic—mutual admiration society. The one coming out five minutes after the other, though both from the ladies. She'd always glommed on to men from the elite realms of genealogically proven power. Not the piddling kind of tabloid tadpole of today that gained rank in the film and television industries by filming themselves smoking crack or, in cahoots with a porn company, releasing an utterly innocent fuck tape. No, she devoured intellectuals and sports Gods alike but was particularly starstruck in the presence of real-deal power. Spurned by world beater—John, she then turned her sights to the up and coming world changer—Bobby. Despite the fact the two had conspired to put her to sleep, for good, perchance to dream.

Others were making the rounds, too. Lesser lights, like Tab Hunter. More famous now for having been a capo in Hollywood's queer mafia than any of his vapid exploits on the silver screen. Ironically, he was even more of a heartbreaker to his male-heterosexual devotees than the female faction of swooning teenyboppers. You could almost hear the collective groan from both camps when Tab got kicked out of the closet. He was still a dreamboat, to Tom's mother, but now even more of a man's man according to his dad. Something he snidely claimed to have known all along.

He's as plastic as my kid sister's old Ken doll, Tom thought. Then, excited by this sudden shard of memory, tried to connect it to something—anything else.
'So, your dad knew Tab was a fag and you had a kid sister with a Ken doll and...? Everybody's kid sister had a Ken doll, you schmuck.'

Tab winked at him as he made a beeline for the little boy's room. Tom toodled back, and they got up to go, ceding their stools to a grateful and sweaty, Fatty Arbuckle. He immediately thought of how many variations there were on the use of a Coke bottle during vaginal sex, traumatic enough to cause death; he'd only known of the one. Did he dent the sides or perforate her bowels perhaps? Miss Rappe was another virtuous actress who agreed to allow the walrus-like film star to indulge his every sexual peccadillo in exchange for a role (probably as an extra) in one of his films. He was more famous for that scandal than any of his disintegrating silent slapstick comedies. Tom probably read about in the same book, on the same toilet that the Dahlia's murder was featured in. He was a wealth of bathroom trivia, stuff he'd forget before the next movement but couldn't remember his surname.

Outside, they were joined by an eager-beaver Dahlia, who quickly slid an arm through Tom's, after being silently rebuffed by Aleister. There was a sudden gust of wind that sounded like the rustle of a fresh bed sheet before floating down and settling on to a giant bed. They looked up to see great black wings silently gliding above them, eclipsing the crescent moon—the same creature Tom had seen from a different aspect. Dahlia gripped Tom's arm even more firmly and buried her face in his shoulder. He liked the attention and thought her pretty in the pictures taken before her run-in with Hollywood. Usually, he was the one ignored or rejected—just knew it, and even though he knew she was using him in anticipation of Aleister picking up the tab for drinks as Tom was his guest, he felt validated now that they were away from an environment that was tainted by people that knew about her shady proclivities. That was the amazing thing, that one was only a second away from looking back at the past. When he looked at the time that way, it frightened him how relentless a thing it was: like watching a freight-train from a standing position roar past you at full-speed.

'Not to worry old chap,' Aleister said, reassuringly, 'They're sentient beings in search of a certain someone, not hunting at random.' He glanced at her as he said this, turned up his collar and dictated a quicker pace. 'That was the Raven, Lightbringer to this place, an indigenous touch, though we're never conscious when the sun does rise.' The fact they were intelligent made the prospect of an encounter that much more frightening. You could almost forgive a shark for mistaking you for a seal; these things might just not like you.

When they arrived at what appeared to be a derelict Chinese restaurant, Aleister compelled them to cut through a blind alley, past a bum begging for spare Shekels. 'Shekels? Tom asked. Dahlia said something about stinking Jews before being shushed by Aleister. They lurched past jittery shadows in cavernous doorways, and others lurking behind dumpsters that seemed itching to jump them. They finally got to a red

door with a window like a ship's portal, hidden in the
recess of a crumbling brick facade. Aleister knocked,
and the door instantly creaked opened. A stern-looking
Chinese man with an old world flourish answered, and
bid them welcome. He had a conspicuous smile, partially
hidden by a wispy Fu-Manchu mustache, and dressed in
a traditional silk jacket, embroidered with a twisting
golden dragon. He led them through the chaos of a
kitchen in the throes of a full-tilt rush. The fare to be
served was not your typical Americanized versions of a
Chinese takeaway, and instead, were confronted by
primordial sea-creatures sat atop two-person platters,
struggling with their monstrous claws against blankets of
silky white sauce. Aleister and his fellow foreigners
were tossed about like bumper cars by the frenzied
kitchen staff as they navigated their way through a
narrow channel between the pass; where noodles and
luminescent slop steamed away under radioactive heat
lamps, and a shuddering dishwasher threatened to
explode. The waiter's jibber-jabber banter at each other
sounded pingy like cartoon gunfire, whizzing past them
and bouncing off the walls, until finally they were
whooshed out the double doors and into the dining room;

driven out by the sheer force of the colonies activity behind them, like interlopers in a busy beehive.

They were seated at a curved and cracked leather banquette, left without menus or the usual accouterments associated with a legitimate restaurant. Tom instinctively ran his fingers along the underside of the table, blindly reading the centuries-worth of wadded-gum that felt to him like bulbous brail or the bumpy surface of a hidden planet. Dahlia spotted a young Nazi sitting all by his lonesome but waited for the bottle to arrive before, like a sucker fish spotting a better host, releasing Tom from her grasp, and torpedoing herself at the hapless soldier, and sticking to him fast, as she had to Tom on the walk over. Aleister poured them drinks, and they clinked their glasses, nodding in a silent toast. Tom motioned again toward his empty pockets.

'No need, my friend,' Aleister said, in a conciliatory tone. 'This evening's on me. The owner is shall we say an ally of mine, and allows me to run a tab, as long as I continue to string him along with some lesser magic. Nothing more than parlor tricks. He's teaching me the bullet catch, though it killed him the last time he performed it.'

Aleister deftly pulled a small coin from behind Tom's ear and pointed to his lapel pocket.

Tom reached in and withdrew a coin identical to the one Aleister had produced.

'Shekels,' Aleister said. 'Ancient Jewish currency. The very same Judas was paid in to betray the Christ and exchanged for what is deemed the value of our lives at our time of death. Some of the denizens, like Dahlia and myself, are degenerate enough to scrape together a little extra, thus allowing us a few earthly amenities beyond the complimentary coffee, pie, and cigarettes.

Aleister and Tom watched as she fawned over the soldier, caressing his hair while pretending to dig his every spitfire proselytization. Aleister continued,

'Some are miserly and hold fast to what they're granted, damned to serving their fate within the relatively safe confines of the diner, but inevitably go mad from boredom. The same madness that comes from having to sit in the waiting room of a dentist's office with only a tattered copies of the same magazines to read over and over again, forever. I've memorized the whole of April 11th, 1954. It was deemed the most uneventful day in history, and thus utterly useless; not even handy for a quick current affair, sports score—God forbid, the weather to liven up a dull conversation of which there are plenty. Some give up and go out with the wild abandon of a condemned man, or a drunken sailor on furlough. Lord knows I've come close myself.'

'What else can you buy, Tom asked?'

'Anything,' Aleister replied. Buy you a sweaty dalliance with the infamous, Black Dahlia.

Tom shook his head, 'No thanks.'

Aleister smiled wickedly. 'Why not? We're impervious to venereal diseases here. Then—'Oh, I see you're married.'

Tom vetted the dull little band around his finger. However, there was nothing to compliment it, just plain fact.

Dahlia was uncomfortable kissing. It wasn't like a hooker's aversion to intimacy. There was no heart or soul left to protect—the tiniest bit of love to spare or share with a special someone. It had been replaced in death and her arrival here, by an animalistic drive to survive. Which she knew was paradoxical because Aleister told her it was, but didn't understand the meaning of this word that described her conundrum perfectly. She wanted to live even though she was already dead. One of her sugar-daddies had taken to treating her like his own personal Eliza Doolittle, after he'd finish his business of buggering her up the ass. He'd go from a shy, retiring professor of philosophy—to a sadistic sodomite; relishing the pain, he wrought within her with his blood-engorged member. Then deflated and sated, he'd immediately transform back into the soft spoken Doctor again, cuddling and stroking, while whispering sweet profundities to her about life and its problems. She couldn't understand a damn thing he was talking about so it must've been his tone that would lull her into a state of foggy fascination and sleepy compliance. Except for one thing the professor screamed mid-orgasm: I think therefore I am. It was so simple yet was more profound and real than any other idea in the whole-wide-world.

To think was to be alive and she happened to like who she was—but couldn't catch a break to save her life. Her last mortal dance, ending in her brutal murder at the hands of that big, dumb sailor, was painful sure, but the suffering was only a matter of moments compared to a lifetime's worth of the shit leading up to the switchblade smile. It was a transition. With her last drop of blood and rattling exhalation, she was jammed on that express train heading here and thinking—Son-of-a-bitch.

She wasn't going to give consciousness up for anybody. So, if she had to turn tricks in this realm like the last to make ends meet to keep the hellhounds at bay—so be it.

This kraut with the bad breath really takes the cake, she thought, as she worked his lips and her specialty—a variety of small-time grifts. Aleister could see behind her seeming impassioned groping was the almost imperceptible movements of an expert pickpocket at work. She was as good at the drop as he was at sleight of hand and coin manipulation—except she had the added advantage of being a woman. However, it seemed from his vantage point that the mark had picked up on her game and instantly turned violent. Exacting the cruelest kind of punishment of all to a disfigured woman—cackling while clawing at the mouth of her mask, and as the last vestige of her disguise fell away, ran his fat finger along the wicked grin carved into her face. The final, gruesome flourish, by her earthly murderer.

Usually, she was able to handle herself in these

inevitable reckonings, tussling with real panache, drawing a frenzied crowd to her and her opponent with her vicious and artful deconstruction both physically and verbally of all comers, the first in line: her jilted johns, who'd tracked her down at the diner. After realizing that her services were a two for one deal: two for her none for them. This fight was different. She wasn't herself, according to Aleister. She wasn't counter-punching (she was infamous for her straight-razor retorts) or defending herself, she just stood there and took it. It was if she'd finally given up, resigned to a fate they were all fighting to avoid. He slapped her stupid and was about to rend her dress from her quivering body when Tom looked to Aleister for guidance—should they intercede on her behalf and possibly subject themselves to an even worse tongue lashing for underestimating her ability to take care of herself? Tom would relish the opportunity to be empowered for the first time since he'd ended up there, rather than a passive witness to the unfolding of this episode of the dream. A hero endowed with superpowers that only existed in fantasies, but never in life. It was the first time since meeting her that he felt sorry for her, that she was a person to be pitied rather than reviled. She would be his dream lover, the archetypal damsel in distress. However, this was only the prologue of what was to come.

Whispery entities, like the long, jagged shadows skulking in the back alley—were flushed out and crept along the floor. They resembled the nightshade that followed the villains in noir films, and took shape, emerging from the dark and dusty corners of the dining room.

The shadow people were the bottom feeders of the spirit world—incubus who fed off the unchecked and diffused sexual energy of freshly pubescent children. Fu used them as muscle and paid them with the end slices of his explosive thoughts during ejaculations. They enveloped the Nazi and roughed him up something fierce, before ejecting him from the after-hours club, head-first, onto the pavement.

Aleister and Tom collected her, gingerly dredging up the dead weight of the once-revered Black Dahlia, as she babbled incessantly about the hellhounds on her trail. They pulled up her underwear and pulled down her dress; wrapped her up in Tom's coat, and hustled her, minus her dignity, out the back door.

Outside, the Nighthawk Express slowed to the speed of a funeral march as it screeched across a skeletal trestle and over the rooftops, showering the street with sizzling sparks as it passed over them. A wolf howled a signal and, an army of paws skittered along the pavement. Dahlia broke free from them and let go with a primordial wail and lament to rival the professional mourners of India. She walked backward with her hands clasped, begging and pleading with Aleister, when the pack suddenly overtook them and began to circle.

Tom picked up a stray piece of pipe and lunged at them, attempting to draw their attention away from the others, as he waited for one of his superpowers to kick in—but maybe, he began to think, then knew, this wasn't a dream.

It was obvious they only wanted the Dahlia. With the swiftness of dried leaves in the autumnal wind, they isolated and closed ranks around her. They snickered at Tom's feeble attempts at heroism—guttural human-like guffaws, that echoed throughout this wasteland of abandoned industry. They were gigantic Dire Wolves, whose speed and dexterity belied their lumbering prehistoric stature. Kings of the mountains of tailings from extinct pit mines. A bridge that had collapsed mid-span, and now resembled a Dada-ist sculpture: the graffiti proclaimed as much.

The Alpha, after the requisite growling and snapping from its henchman, distinguished itself by rising from all fours and making itself bipedal. It stepped forth with the noble comportment of a King and the spooked, steely approach of a deadly predator; ready to pounce at any second. It came chest to nose with a surprisingly cool Aleister and bent down to address him, enshrouding his head with its hot breath as it spoke.

'The Raven awaits, Aleister. Don't tempt my ambition to bring him three instead of the one,' it said, in a molten growl. 'And kindly tell your partner to put down his pesky stick. We are not lowly dogs in want of a game of fetch.'

Aleister reluctantly obeyed, wresting the bar from Tom, and ignoring his protestations, tossed it into the gutter. Dahlia yanked Aleister by the lapels and pulled him close, 'Please Al, don't let them take me. Don't let them put me to sleep!' Hell is different for everyone, Aleister thought, as they tore her from them. As for Dahlia's version? She told him once after he'd succumbed to a belly full of Fu's bathtub gin and her pleas to whisper sweet profundities in her ear. They were smoking cigarettes, wishing the memory of what had just passed between them would evaporate like the smoke. She said it would be an unthinking, unblinking awareness of her suffering without end.

With one swipe of its claw, her dress was sheared from her body, exposing her patchwork chest to the panting Betas, whose steaming pink baculum dripped with anticipation for the feed. They wolf-whistled, and Tom gasped. 'The scars,' he whispered with the awe of a believer bearing witness to the unveiling of a holy relic.

She looked like one of the Frankenstein monster's go-to girlfriends, cowering from the fire in their eyes as they slowly closed in. Aleister and Tom lowered their gaze in anticipation of the slaughter to come. They refused to watch but could hear crystal-clear, her torment as the Alpha brutally raped her, mounting her as all dogs do—from behind, working its hindquarters like a piston, biting her neck and growling, while she yelped. Then sated, unceremoniously cast her to the Betas, who took turns having their way with her raggedy body.

Play dead, Dahlia. Play dead, for fuck sakes, they

thought, knowing the beasts would continue the assault whether she was dead or alive. After they'd finished ravaging her and tearing her apart at the seams, Tom nudged Aleister and pointed to her remains—now no more than a smoking heap of tattered clothing, beside a desecrated corpse, marinating in a shimmering pool of arterial blood and motor oil.

Suddenly, the belly started to undulate in rhythmic ripples of flesh. As if thousands of maggots had invaded her stomach and were mounting an assault on the rest of her corpse. The waves turned to claws cleaving at the walls of her rubbery, distended abdomen. Then, as if delivered cesarean by invisible hands, a wolf cub burst forth from her womb, and shakily presented itself before the Betas, who greedily licked the afterbirth from its lithe body.

After they'd finished cleaning her, they dragged her human carcass to the concrete base of a disused electrical tower that would act as a quick and dirty altar and waited for the Raven. The newborn wolf stayed behind for a moment, and said with snarling, dripping fangs, what she knew would be her last human utterance before being cast out to serve as the pack's bitch in hell.

'We'll meet again, Al. I'll be the big bad wolf with the long sharp teeth. The better to rip that limp dick clean off, my dear.'

With that blood oath, she bounded off to join the others, and Aleister and Tom watched, as on great black wings it came. It's silhouette shuttering the full moon as it swooped down and plucked the wolves tribute with talons that flashed and scraped like scythes. They howled as indeed a raven, the size of a Lincoln SUV, regarded them all with glistening, unblinking, satellite dish-sized eyes, then took flight, and perched itself atop a barbed-wire nest, regurgitating the flesh from Dahlia's corpse to it's squawking young.

Aleister grabbed Tom and drug him away, not bothering with an explanation, as one adequate to the task could not possibly be provided right now, if ever. More importantly—the blackout was looming, and the wolves had now turned their attention to them and were discussing something that might involve violating the slippery rules of this place. Besides, how do you lament or explain the unfathomable to a complete neophyte?

'What's the Raven's problem, giant cat got its tongue?' said Tom to himself, then giggled madly. The man is cracking up, Aleister worried. You might as well try to explain the concept of self-loathing to a Buddhist or the merit of a Jackson Pollock to Michelangelo.

They made it back to the Diner, just beating the blackout. They scooched into a window booth beside some guy that Tom swore was L Ron Hubbard, and one of the Roswell greys (the pilot responsible for the crash), and a man who looked like a broken vacuum cleaner salesman from the fifties. They drifted into an uncomfortable silence and waited for the stupor to wash over them. Aleister relished this stage, what he called the taste of dragon smoke, as the effect was somewhat like that of really good opium. A decades-long habit that had turned to morphine, then heroin. He did finally kick the habit—albeit involuntarily on his deathbed. Then they were gone, out like lights, lost in a dreamless sleep—like death.

Chapter 4

Father Kilty, quaffed the last of his morning whiskey, killing the vapor at the bottom of his chalice, then making sure with one last wheezy inhalation. He chased it with a gulp of astringent mouthwash and got lost in his reflection in the mirror. It was empty, and so was Kilty.

He had formed without content. Born a ghost. He'd used this vacuity and his photographic memory to his advantage scholastically. With his uncanny ability to regurgitate facts and figures at will, or rather, at the behest of his teachers, he was assured class valedictorian honors through each successive stage of his education, and the enmity of his classmates and future peers.

The boy never had an independent thought or feeling and tried anything to generate one of the latter, starting by ripping the wings and legs from sluggish window flies, and watching intently as the torsos buzzed and span in directionless trajectories. However, still, there was nothing. No sympathy for the vile creatures, as he reasoned—he'd never had his appendages ripped off.

He was hollow. It was this complete inability to socialize with his classmates that earned him the moniker, 'numbnuts' to his face, but something far more derogatory with his back turned.

His only friend was the parish priest who also acted in the capacity of spiritual advisor, marriage counselor, sex-ed teacher, basketball coach, and overall figurehead to the students and faculty; replete with a bronze bust of his bull-head in the school foyer. The priest was astounded by Kilty's ability to recite the bible chapter and verse, and took him under his wing as his protege and eventually, with some grooming—lapdog. He encouraged him to pursue the priesthood as a vocation and assured Kilty that if he played his cards right, with his gifts, he could ascend the vaunted heights of the Catholic church and eventually—God willing, the Papacy.

His descent began in earnest when Kilty earned the coveted position of the head altar boy and bell ringer during mass. The boy first felt the cunning allure of absolute power, when with the invocation of the Holy Spirit, while seemingly under the sway of the same possession as the Charismatic faction of the parishioners, he would watch as they swooned and speak in tongues. While barely restraining themselves from ripping off his clothes and writhing on the floor—co-catalyst for the fundamentalists in their orgiastic reverie. He was the Magus's apprentice in a Catholic version of a black mass, sounding the bells for the conjuration, binding, and banishment of the demon after the ritual.

THE CONJURATION

Come forth Gaap! Oh, great demon hear my plea. I call thee up by the power of this circle and by thy own most secret name Gaap. Appear now that I may have council with thee. I conjure thee ancient demon without fear and trembling. Come forth and manifest thyself within me.

Kilty's binding began with his first confession. The good Father encouraged him to sit face to face with him in persona Christi as the confessional box was for cowards. Once the rite began, the priest bade him come, come closer, my child, until finally, he was sitting on the priest's lap.

THE BINDING

You are most welcome, Oh great demon Gaap, I have called thee forth by ancient rites, and I now bind thee here within me until thou hast answered all my questions and diligently performed my will."

The creeping, crawling—fumbling hands of his confessor, made Kilty sick to his stomach and caused him to stifle vomit every time—and ever more frequently. So much so that he was forced to manufacture sins while withholding his coerced participation in the most diabolical of them all.

However, he could about tolerate these violations of the former sanctity of his body with the sneaky gift of wine from the vestry, and the subtle intimations of the dire consequence s if he didn't comply completely—but then, just barely. The thought of being stripped of his office and the attendant benefits of his unholy alliance made him feel something for the very first time—a gnawing, twisting anguish in his brain. The place he kept spartan and orderly; once a library for his collected data, and now the receptacle for this one feeling—enmeshed with the blackest of secrets seeping the stuff of rain drenched ashtrays into his soul. Kilty swore a blood oath to one day smote the diddler with the very demon he bound in service to hold sway over his tidy little fiefdom. However, until then, he would have to grin and bear his penance of 666 Our Fathers, Hail Marys, and an Act of Contrition. There would be no forgiveness or mercy on anyone, ever. Little did he know that this absolute power that he yearned for, and one day wield, would not only corrupt him, but subsequent generations of innocents to come, including Tom, and Tom's son.

Now Kilty wracked his brain for the banishment, and the burial place of the demon's talisman, but in old age, and decrepitude accelerated by his vices, the former facility for memorization was failing him, and as a result, he was unable to banish the demon back to the abode whence it came. Thus he was unaware of the truth—that the demon had nothing to do with his appetites. He thought the only respite from Gaap's influence was gotten from drinking, and this he did in ever increasing increments over the day. However, it was taking its toll, not only on his health but his ability to maintain enough discretion to keep the prying eyes of the church, and the whispers of the parishioners that caused this new scrutiny at bay. Hence he was assigned a church-appointed minder. Just as a precaution, he was assured by his Bishop—to keep the Philistines off our backs—nothing to worry about, John.

He checked his once long, lustrous hair, now grey, greasy and matted, finger-combed the beginnings of its slow devolution into dreadlocks (he now resembled a junkie Jesus), his breath in his hand, and proceeded out of the modest rectory to give an audience to the dwindling faithful, gathered at the foot of the porch.

In the meantime, he performed his priestly duties with perfunctory professionalism. However, that once beloved, shit-eating grin, was now regarded as wicked by the skeptics and his anonymous accusers. He shook hands, pecked mother's and their babies on the cheek (careful not to linger too long), and disappeared into the sacristy to prepare to preach to the great unwashed.

Father Martin, his new minder accompanied him; a retired cop—turned priest, then investigator, for the archdiocese version of internal affairs. The constant surveillance was making Kilty irritable and prevented him from engaging in his other means of release. This too contributed to his erratic behavior of late, and longer, more suspicious glances from the inquisitor, who was also given the onerous task of monitoring Kilty's use of his laptop (which was locked up at night), his contact with the altar boys, any church-related affairs, and to accompany Kilty on his sojourns into the city.

Kilty knew if he played the long game of possum convincingly enough, he'd soon be left to his vices, and the demon would begin the meticulous and time-consuming process of grooming another protege. This, to replace the old one, who no longer tickled his fancy, as his advancing age (he was going on twelve), was robbing him of his baby-faced allure. Failing that, he'd merely have his boys take care of Martin, as they had the last—rat bastard.

The boys were growing impatient with the constant presence of the interloper—Father Martin. Serving mass wasn't as much fun as it had been under the exclusive regime and tutelage of Father Kilty, and they were itching to do something about it. Since he'd started his vigil, Martin had put an end to the distribution of tributary cigarettes, theft of sacramental wine, gambling, and subterranean sexual experimentation that took place in the church basement after a condensed mass, and the geriatric tea and biscuit crowd had cleared out. The boys were never severely punished for their sins; just given slaps on the wrist, and excruciating impromptu sex talks by the naive, but surprisingly well versed Martin. He even went so far as to admonish the petty practice of group masturbation as a mortal sin. If only he'd seen what lay behind the false wall, they thought, after he'd finished his lectures, and told them as a consolation for their time, to go ahead, and help themselves to as many cookies as they liked.

Michael, his head altar boy, caught Father Kilty alone and unawares, startling the priest as he gently put his hand on his back.

'You all right John?'

Kilty turned around to reveal his sad—bloodshot eyes, and sighed. 'You can't call me that Michael, just for now. That's the kind of thing he's looking for to put in his report to the Bishop.'

'Yes, John—I mean Father,' Michael replied, exaggerating his hurt for being shunned, but secretly relieved.

Michael hated himself for still caring about the man guilty of twisting his brain into thinking he might be a faggot, or something even more monstrous like Kilty was. How could he be, though, he wondered? Because whenever he was free from Kilty's furtive eyes and sticky grasp, he'd be secretly courting his true love; his latest girl crush—the super-cute Elaine Williams, plying her with tchotchkes he'd steal from his grandmother's display cabinet, in exchange for hugs and promises. The only thing that worked to quell his nauseating confusion was the wine, but there would be none of that relief today, as the snoopy Father Martin was looming around every corner, doggedly trying to catch them out. So he got a case of the busys instead. Busy hands and a racing mind silenced the madrigal of ceaseless chatter in his head, and prevented the demon from burrowing into his brain, and creating a permanent nesting place there. He watched himself in the mirror as he discreetly slipped on his cassock and readied the altar for mass. Lastly fetching the bible from the holy place where only the high priest and he could go and read from it. It was a confused compendium of Grimoires and Gnostic gospels that had been discarded by Warlocks and the Council of Nicaea. Considered a hindrance to establishing continuity in the story of Jesus and maintaining the newly organized church as a patriarchal oligarchy—eliminating women as key players in its evolution and maintenance, reducing them to tertiary characters in the greatest story ever told.

Kilty's favorite was the gospel of Judas. The most reviled baddie in history. In a reveal to rival Dallas's—*Who Shot J.R?* He delighted in his masterful insinuation of Judas as the real hero of the biblical canon, sacrificing his legacy to act as the vital cog in the eventual resurrection, the lynchpin of Catholicism. The utterance of his name now reduced to an acceptable alternative to Jesus as a curse word, and the name of

Michael's least favorite heavy metal band.

Kilty didn't give a shit about the biblical ladies posthumous reputations, and nobody noticed his subterfuge. The congregation preoccupied with coveting their neighbor's husbands or wives while speaking in tongues to protest. Martin only cared about catching him in a vile act, cutting his balls off and force-feeding them to the bastard.

Gaap was tired, too. Fed up this possession. Exhausted from slaking the wheezy, cancer-riddled, geriatric husk of a body, that was now Kilty's corporeal temple. His sedentary, chain-smoking, dipsomaniacal existence having taken its toll on his attractiveness, virility, and therefore his usefulness. However, it was his dependence on viagra to get a hard-on that was the real kicker. He was either going to have to trade him in for a newer model or wait for Michael to grow up and assume his rightful place as Kilty's heir to the presider's chair, thus guaranteeing him cock-on-tap for the next forty years or so.

Gaap's dilemma was that he'd been bound but not banished by Kilty, and therefore was trapped, like a genie in a plugged bottle, and forbidden to possess other—more viable practitioners of black magic. As he specialized in intensifying love or hatred, he'd rocketed to the top of the demon charts (he was one of 72 daemons in the Goetia) for a record three consecutive centuries, and only dropped out of the top ten when that bitch—Paris Hilton, stole his idea for the whole-frenemy thing. Gene Simmons pulled a similar fast one on Mammon, the Demon who influences money and power by copyrighting the money bag symbol before Mam had gotten around to it. Gaap had already punished her by affecting a judge to throw her in prison for forty-five days on a trumped-up charge for violating her probation. So now he was going to further her torment by compelling her to work as a farmhand with her 'frenemy'—Nicole Richie and having it filmed for a reality t.v series, killing two insipid dodos with one stone. He was also in secret talks with the MTV brass to develop another reality series tentatively titled *Celebrity Rehab*, a sort of clearinghouse for his D-listers who constantly pestered him for favors and used up their fifteen minutes of fame. He was good. Must've been head of a network in a past life, he thought, whistling the Love Boat theme as he toddled off to his next appointment.

Satan was bored. Dominion over the earth and the squirming larvae that blighted its surface was nearly as dull as the utopic heaven he'd been cast out from—and so to was Omnipotence. He'd broken the news about enlightenment to a few Buddhists in hell, but was left wanting by their total indifference to this revelation and seeming immunity to the infernal suffering he inflicted upon them.

One such Zen monk, who'd specifically requested to fry in hell, had even asked at one point to be turned over, being done on that side. What the fuck? He thought, as he inhaled deeply from a spit-soaked, fire log sized stogie. He didn't get it. This guy was a real Buddhist, not the garden variety-granola eating, dope smoking, yoga matt wielding kind, mind you, but the died-in-the-wool variety, who wouldn't say shit if their mouth was full of it—condemned to hell? Just because they were atheists, come on. However, that was God for you. Hell, he'd been cast out merely for expressing his desire for a little equality with the old man.

His only source of amusement now was what he

considered to be his inalienable right to fuck with his constituency. So as a distraction from the eternal tedium, he appointed himself the first ever black Mayor of Gristle Arkansas. The most racist town in America, and therefore the world.

'Time to stir us up some shit, son,' he chortled to the Sheriff on his right; as he insolently ashed on the freshly polished floor of the gymnasium, strutted on up to the lectern, and commenced with his acceptance speech before the thunderstruck citizenry. 'Now you listen here...'

What in tarnation, they thought. The toothless faces, frozen in paralytic shock, and their moonshine-soaked brains in feeble-minded, telepathic unity.
How the hell did some great big, greasy nigger suddenly become Mayor of our perfectly backward little town?

One of them, an old crone who'd been sipping from a battered aluminum hip-flask, checked around the cork to see if they were dealing with an escaped genie or such. The others looked back at the lily-white, chicken-headed man dressed in his Sunday best. An all-white combo befitting the occasion; the twenty-gallon stetson perched atop an itchy-sounding polyester leisure suit. The candidate they thought they'd voted into office and had religiously, for the last ten terms. Wait a goddamn' minute. Wasn't that, it couldn't be Earnest Scrub, the rag and bone man from yonder Cripple Creek road? The devil's teeth rolled out like the ivories on a ragtime piano.

'Dat be me-cha-cha-cha!'

'Folks, I stand here before you because to quote that great jew, Robert Zimmerman, better known as Bobby Dylan, 'the times they are-a-changin.' His first mayoral proclamation bellowed—straight from the rot-guts and his host Earl Scrub's bluesy-growl of a holler.

Chapter 5

It was Michael and Jeff's turn to walk Elaine home. There was an unspoken, loosey-goosey, system in place, typical of children, whereby they recognized the pecking order and waited their turn to woo the prettiest and most popular girl in school. She sent hearts-a-flutter and gave boys and girls alike the whirly-birds in their love distended tummies. She had short-cropped, white blonde hair that seemed a waste of its shimmer to have cut into such a boyish fashion. Her school skirt was worn high enough above the knees for all to see that she preferred rough and tumbled to girly gossip and playing house. Michael's best friend, Jeff; a native American boy who was afflicted by Gigantism was allowed to accompany them, lumbering along amiably enough, though he liked her too. He wouldn't dare jockey for position or try any funny stuff like the other guys out of respect for his friendship with Michael and his 'golden boy' status within the parish. This and the knowledge from experience that her parents would frown on her commiserating with a 'no-good Indian.' A boy whose Father, Cecil Gaylord, (raising Jeff in his delinquent mother's stead) was regarded as a drugged-out, pagan-savage by the other families, but passed himself off as a harmless, peace-loving casualty of the sixties, who had more liberal-leaning attitudes about the raising of his sons. Yes, it's true from time to time he indulged in the occasional toke from the hand-carved implement he referred to as his peace pipe and was a born-again Pescatarian, but this didn't warrant his complete ostracization from the other parents. If only they knew the half of it…

Today they planned on finally initiating Elaine into their fledgling secret society in a ceremony they'd concocted, consisting of; speculating on the questionable heterosexuality of the mannish second-grade teacher: specific to just what such abominations entailed, and other gossipy musings, choking on hand-rolled cigarettes, listening to Led Zeppelin, inventing a means whereby they could listen to CD's backwards to hear the subliminal messages, and being toyed with by the Ouija board.

Jeff had recently gotten this handcrafted beauty blessed or super-charged as he called it (thus imbuing it with higher power) by the ex-hippie and wannabe Wiccan witch who lived in a hobbit cottage at the end of the cul-de-sac. According to her, his Dad had been a bit of a sly guru and had taught her a trick or two back in the days when curiosity in Magick (as Gaylord's former master spelled it) revived as an alternative to the conservative dogma of their post-nuclear parent's belief systems. Both by the naive hippies (none more unhygenic or filthy in other ways than Esmeralda according to Gaylord) and bored, typically affluent, student- intellectuals, driven by a desire to be freed from the repressive beliefs of their fore-bearers and explore in earnest the forbidden areas of sex, drugs, with a liberal dose of rock and roll thrown in to liven up the whole hootenanny. Esmeralda was considered a harmless eccentric by her neighbors, a casualty of the sixties by the community at large, and a devil worshipping whore of the devil by the church, who might as well have had her excommunicated her for the shoddy way they treated her during the Yuletide season.

When she opened the door, Jeff's senses got assaulted by a potpourri of odors that smelled like the registration desk at a convention for octogenarians, and she, to put it mildly, was a shambles—tinkling like a wind chime with every melodramatic gesture. Talismans and trinkets jangled from every part of her body; from the top of her greasy hot-mess tangle of fried brown hair to the bangles that dangled on her spindly spider-like arms, right down to the pinky rings on her dirty little toes.

'Jeff,' she said, a nub of a doobie threatening to burn her lips, then did.

'Hey.'

She ushered him into her lair: a veritable temple dedicated to angels, goblins, and garden gnomes. Her breasts were as saggy as the bookshelves overloaded with the coffee table variety of picture book on Wicca, feminism, and hydroponics. Empty wine bottles and a tv transformed into drippy candle holders, and vinyl LP's had become convenient ashtrays and drink coasters. Lastly, stinky cat-litter boxes in every pee-stained corner of the room.

He was in a state of complete sensory overload and could only imagine the chaos of her mind. She shifted around some junk and invited him to take a seat somewhere. She motioned for the thing tucked under his arm which he withdrew from a heavy metal t-shirt. She was awestruck.

'Wow man, that is some fucking cool-ass board.'

'Thanks,' he said, in his usual stoic manner.

'What's it made from?'

'Cherrywood. The toughest,' he replied, with beaming pride.

'Sure is,' she said, nodding in agreement.

'May I?' She fired up another pinner joint.

He handed it over with the dourness he thought befitted a holy relic. She examined the ouija's every nook and jagged cranny, running a bony finger along every letter and number before pronouncing her expert appraisal. 'Bitchin, dude. So you want it blessed, eh?'

'Supercharged,' he stated affirmatively.

She handed it back to him. ' You talked to any spirits yet?'

'Yup, a couple. One-goes by Helen. Her pictures on that disk in the cover of the Led Zeppelin three album and the other was an…, Aleister Crow, something.'

At the latter spirits name her scrunched, bloodshot eyes, widened with fear.

'Pretty badass for a newbie,' she said. 'He's a real heavy-hitter in the spirit world. Fuck you right up, if you're not careful.'

'Awesome,' he smiled.

She looked at him skeptically. 'You sure your dad said this was ok?'

'Yup.'

She got up. 'All right then, let me get my thing-a-ma-jigs, then.' She leaped over one of the errant litter boxes and ducked under a dreamcatcher before disappearing behind a beaded curtain. After an explosion of cranging from the back room, she re-appeared bearing a box painted crudely with the epithet: Esmeralda's

Magical Doo-Dads. Then kneeling and creaking it open, revealed its contents: a battered tin cup, bundle of sage, a little black book of shadows, and some other mundane-looking objects: a melange of incongruent miscellany, strewn about its purple velvet-lined insides.

The baptism itself struck Jeff as corny. A lot of airy-fairy, mumbo-jumbo, hocus-pocus-type—shit. She throat-sung incomprehensible incantations, while two-fisting bushels of lavender and sage, wafting them in his face. The dense, perfumed smoke and her repetitive rocking made him feel seasick, and therefore unable to concentrate fully on the ceremony, thinking he might get a rough idea of the process and then go into the supercharging business for himself.

Suddenly, her buggy eyes popped open, and she shuddered awake from her trance. She was sweaty, and a tuft of hair with one of the dangly bits was plastered to her forehead as if she'd just flopped back on to the bed after strenuous sex. 'Donesky,' she said, as she handed back the board. Jeff didn't seem entirely convinced as he dropped a plastic lunch baggie of weed in her hand.

'Gracias, kiddo,' she said but noticed the hint of skepticism in his eyes.

'Listen, you may not dig my brand of magic, but remember, there's no such thing as wrong—only different, kay?'

'Thanks, Es, catch you later,' he said, as he sprinted home, and straight to the woodshed, he'd converted into a makeshift temple to try out its new super-charged awesomeness.

She may have been a kook, but he had to admit that overall her brand of hoodoo-light seemed to work. He no longer had to lay hands on the planchette for it to move, and there was a shitload of poltergeist activity—long after the spirits were banished. The most persistent being a spirit by the name of Aleister Crowley, who claimed to be immortalized on the cover of The Beatles: *Sargent Pepper's Lonely Hearts Club Band.*

As Gaylord's only semi-coherent adept, one of Esmeralda's jobs besides entertaining his grandson Jeff, was to rescue his newspaper from the rain, give him the heads-up when Aleister was afoot, and certain other discreet services. As he no longer toyed with such childish conveyances as spirit boards and the tarot, he counted on her to let him know if Aleister was making rumblings about returning from the dead, and she did so, telepathically.

Even though, in Aleister's current state, his power was limited to that of the unnoticeable movements of small objects, shadowy—corner of the eye manifestations, and low-level wattage; the equivalent of static electricity, he couldn't take any chances. Aleister would stop at nothing until he'd gotten his precious codex back from Gaylord's clutches. The only extant, authentic copy of the *Goetia: The Lesser Key of Solomon.*

The author, Abramelin the mage, was reputed to have been an Egyptian magus who taught Abraham of Worms this system of magic, later incorporated by the Golden Dawn (a magical society young Aleister was a member of) into their rituals. They claimed that the demons evoked from the book had aided King Solomon, in the construction of his fabled temple.

Regarded as the most powerful and dangerous magic known to man, some succeeded in binding the demons within to do their bidding, but most went mad or perished from the experience.

A tawdry paperback titled the *Necronomicon* had made the rounds of high-school libraries and been circulated by stoned students for decades. It was claimed by the publisher to be a reprint of the of the original Goetia, but was just a ghostwritten fake, dreamt up by the perennially broke fantasy writer, H.P Lovecraft.

Aleister claimed his copy was written in the blood, and bound in the skin of newborn babies. Gaylord called bullshit, but it was great for a story, and the things value amongst collectors and antiquarian booksellers. The guitarist from that wretched rock band, Led Zeppelin, an avid collector of Crowleyania, and former owner of Aleister's Boleskine House on the Scottish Loch, had somehow gotten Gaylord's number and made a substantial monetary offer, but this was not what he was after, for money when truly desired was easily obtained.

When asked how it had gotten into his possession, Gaylord wove an elaborate tale of his friendship and collaboration with the great Crowley, and how he'd gifted it to him for his years of devotion and service as his personal secretary. But in actual fact, had stolen it from him in Egypt, when Aleister had his back turned to him during one of the interminably-long, transmission sessions, and was subsumed in a trance-state, transcribing what would go onto become: *The Book of the Law*, as dictated by the deities Nuit, Hadit, and, Ra-Hoor—something or other.

Now, after having spent decades protecting it from an endless procession of covetous magi, Gaylord was finally on the cusp of brokering a deal with Satan, that would see him be the first to achieve conversation and knowledge of his holy guardian angel—Aleister's life's purpose, 'whatever the hell that meant,'Gaylord would scoff. He only hoped it wasn't the Buddhist brand of enlightenment (that struck him as a whole lot of nothingness), but most important, as a part of the package deal; he would be granted the recently vacated position as Satan's hitman of humans: The Santa Morte, God of Death.

His predecessor had been a Mexican woman with a fiery disposition, who'd done a serviceable enough job, but was averse to the killing of innocents, so demoted herself to a domestic position within the hierarchy.

The conversation and knowledge would be the final kick in the teeth to Aleister, his former subjugator. However, Gaylord's real endgame was power. A power that knew no bounds: could not be demarcated, or even defined, and there was none greater than to be tasked with the snuffing-out of human lives. Gaylord's wishes were considered base and easily granted by the lesser demons. Whereas Aleister pursued the altruistic goal of awakening, despite his youthful assertion that he was 'the wickedest man in the world' and a reincarnation of the biblical, 'Great Beast of Revelation.' The ritual required much suffering, and often many lifetimes to achieve. Hence Gaylord's decision to take a well-trodden shortcut, and make a deal with the devil.

The call had come out of the blue. On an evening that he was scheduled to MC a screening of a restored print of Kenneth Anger's *Lucifer Rising*, at the second-run theatre he owned in a shady part of the city. He didn't care for it particularly, preferring a classic Hollywood narrative to this kind of experimental claptrap. However, it was good for a quick buck and a draw for the goths that had taken over the slum around the cinema, while he waited for the major theatre chains hand me downs and cast offs.

He was told by one of the ushers that he had an urgent phone call and took it in the projection booth. A man with a chewing tobacco-thick, southern drawl, introduced himself as Earnest Scrub, acting Mayor of

Gristle Arkansas, and Satan's emissary. He was interested in making a deal for the Goetia, and asked if Gaylord was keen on the idea? 'Absolutely? Fair enough,' Mayor Scrub said, and would call back at a later date to make arrangements for the exchange. Conversation and blah, blah, blah of gaylord's whatever, and the Smith and Wesson .500, handgun of death, for the book—straight up.

In the meantime, he'd have to watch his back and Jeff's. He knew the little shit had started to experiment with magic (he would have preferred the typical, hogging of the bathroom with hours-long masturbation sessions, or marijuana), but had instinctively encouraged the pissing about with the I Ching, Ouija, and Gaylord's old Tarot cards. They were nothing but harmless little amusements to him, but could potentially be used as access points to get to Gaylord, and Aleister was not above fiddling with his son to achieve this end.

He checked himself in the black mirror to make sure his bald pate was perfectly smooth, scented, and shiny; pulled his meticulously groomed goatee to a point, and arched the eyebrow he used as a wicked inquisitor. Satisfied with the devilish persona he'd cultivated for over a century, he opened the door to Esmeralda — who was just about to knock and ushered her inside for his weekly spanking. He was naked but for rubber ducky incontinent pants and a sheepish grin. 'I been a bad boy,' he said.

She reeked of patchouli and roach-ends but was damned good at administering corporal punishment to centenarians without breaking brittle bones. For though Gaylord had cast an eternal virility spell on himself it did nothing to stunt the aging process, and when he made love, he groaned and creaked like an old pirate ship in dry dock.

Chapter 6

Jeff led them to the woodshed; tucked under an ancient Willow, and hidden from view behind a curtain of its weeping branches—like the little Cezanne Gaylord had gotten for a steal many moons ago. Michael had managed to lure Elaine, the reluctant truant, into their hermitage with the promise of showing her something really and truly out of this world. The place stunk of stale cigarettes and weed because it doubled as Jeff's big brother's, headbanger's hot-box. It did have a certain spooky charm, though, as Gaylordl had given Jeff some old movie posters and lobby cards from classic horror pictures to decorate the fort.

Helen, the first spirit Jeff had ever made contact with, before the board had been super-charged, hung around for a while but had been forced out it seemed, by the more powerful Aleister, whose favorite trick was to fire the planchette clear across the room when Jeff had the temerity to banish him at the end of sessions.

The brothers eventually gave up on the shed as their man cave after experiencing one, too, many creepy, paranormal-type incidents. The oldest, Vinnie, even claimed that he'd been smacked in the face by an invisible hand when he made the mistake of putting on one of his Dad's, scratchy-old blues records.

Jeff plugged in the boom-box and put on a Led Zeppelin CD on low, to enhance the eerie vibe, then pulled up old Coca-Cola crates around a candle wax encrusted industrial spool. He pried back a loose floorboard and pulled out the ouija, showing it to the others with the gestures of a magician about to pull a rabbit from his empty top hat, then placed it gently on the table.

'What's that?' Elaine asked, scrunching her nose at the bundled up Judas Priest t-shirt.

'Judas Priest?' Michael asked, incredulously.

'It's was the guy's next door, man,' Jeff answered, unwrapping the board and placing the planchette on the gleeful corner greeting: Hello! 'He was giving it away.'

'What's that?' She asked again. It turns out she was more annoying than pretty and was probably going to 'What's that?' them to death.

'No more questions,' Jeff said testily, as he lit a stubby black candle, squinted his eyes, and focused intently on the planchette, willing it to move.
'Don't we have to put our fingers on it or something?' Michael asked, motioning to do so. Jeff put up his hand,'Not anymore, it's super-charged,' and told them to concentrate.

'On what?'

After the 'gay' part of *Stairway to Heaven* had segued into the 'cool' section, the planchette began to strain against gravity; its posts scraping painfully against the grain of the wood, first down, and then sharply back up to the greeting—*HELLO*. It booted from the corner with the swiftness of a speed skater on fresh ice and spelled out the name: *J-E-F-F.* Then eased off, as if rounding the corner—*LOOKY-LOO.* Now it was moving so fast, and with such enthusiasm, that it was leaving skid-marks as it burned out and fish-tailed around the characters. The spirit was obviously frustrated by the limitations of this mode of communication, and so Elaine, tasked with scribbling down whatever was being said by the board, abandoned the notepad entirely, and just allowed the whispery voice in her head to resonate, and give it shout with her shrill-sounding larynx.

'I never thought I'd say this but, thank God for mediums,' she said, with a jaunty, British accent.

'Aleister? Jeff asked, excitedly, looking to Michael for recognition of the momentousness of the moment.

'Motherfucking, super-charged—told you!' Jeff squealed.

However, Michael was too busy examining the change in Elaine's body and demeanor, to honor Jeff's achievement. In an instant, her face had slackened from its usual glowing innocence and taut, porcelain-like perfection, to a jowly head, ravaged but wizened by decades of debauchery. Her body seemed to bloat as well. Michael's eyes strayed down to her once perky breasts that now sagged like flat old-man tits and her belly jiggled, as it runneth over her skirt.

'Tis I, Jeffrey,' she tittered, her eyes afire with new life and lust for more of it. 'It's a start, Jeffy boy!' Then pointing to a corner of the room too dark for shadows, bellowed,

'Looky-loo.' Suddenly, the candle flared like a torch, all the way to the patchwork roof, licking the tinder-dry shingles, and the dark began to dance and take shape.

'Seances are so much more expeditious than prayers,' she quipped, its form coalescing into a wraith-like apparition. As its power grew, so too, she seemed to drain of hers, and the spirit that inhabited her began to individuate from its host. Slowly she slumped down to the ground: first twisting and writhing on the dirt floor, then stiffening and jerking about in a violent fit, shooting tendrils of spit from her contorted mouth like an epileptic in the throes of a grand mal seizure. Michael, jumped up and knelt beside her, jamming his hand into her mouth to pull her slithering tongue out from the back of her throat, but yanked it out, just as she bit down with a force that would've cut his fingers—clean off. Jeff, just sat there, watching the whole thing unfold, grinning and smashing his hands together like the tin symbols of a manic, wind-up monkey, and when the bedlam began to settle, stopped in sections, as his internal spring unwound. To him, it was the greatest phantasmagorical shit-show on earth.

The apparition glided over to Jeff; seething, looming, and lingering over him for a moment as if contemplating the prospect of possessing him before it burst out the shuttered window behind him. A gale-force gust blew out the candle, and parted his bangs, leaving only a profound quiet, and echoing laughter in its stead. The song had finished, and the gentle strains of the beginning were supposed to start again.

All was deathly still, and the candle smoke drifted lazily upward then dispersed into nothingness. The stereo blared white noise. Elaine was the first to move, scraping the heels of her penny loafers along the ground as she drew her legs underneath her and sat up. Her beautiful hair was frazzled, and blood caked at the corners of her trembling mouth. 'What happened?' She asked, looking dumbly to the boys for an explanation. Michael smoothed down her hair and gave her a tissue gesticulating at her to clean her face.

'Nothing, Elaine. Absolutely nothing, kay?' he said grimly.

'Kay...I gotta go now, okay?'

'Okay. 'Michael brought her to her feet and pushed her out the door without saying goodbye. Aleister followed closely on their heels, a shadow within Michael's silhouette, creeping along the moonlit pavement.

He dropped her at home. She offered him her cheek for a kiss, but he demurred.

Sometimes people are prettier from a faraway place, he thought, his newfound disinterest only serving to spark hers. Their roles reversed, she would have to make an appointment if she wanted to walk him home. At least it would spare him the chore of having to come up with an explanation for the mysterious disappearance of his Grandma's favorite crystal unicorn.

When he got home there was a police car in the driveway, and two plainclothes officers in the foyer. They were awkwardly consoling his Mother. His stepfather was dead.

Tom, as Michael had insisted on calling him, had

thrown himself in front of a subway train on his way home from work. It looked like it was going to be ruled a suicide. There was no note or tears from Michael. Aleister detached himself and continued inside.

He glided through the stoic police officers and Michael's aggrieved mother but had to stay close to the wall because the foyer—lit with blistering spotlights, eradicated any subtle, comforting darksome he associated with these areas in a real homey-home. Aleister hurried down the hallway, and his sense memory was assailed by acid. A searing, lemon fresh astringency. It was even more potent than the stuff the coroner had used to chase away the smell of death after he'd finished Aleister's autopsy. He followed the cheap, snap-together, vinyl flooring into the kitchen and it was spotless. The appliances shone with a brightness that made him conclude that nothing was ever cooked fresh in this kitchen, and was proven correct when he put his head through the ice-box and found it heaving with healthy-alternative frozen meals, and not so much as a lowly egg in the fridge. He shot up through the ceiling into the master bedroom. It was barren, and he wondered how Michael had ever come into existence. It was sparsely equipped with faux-wood, big-box store furniture, and dominated by a bed that looked like a hovering slab. He'd never lower himself to fuck in that thing, he thought. Then he spotted it, the lone framed picture in the house, on the bedside table. He bent down to look at it as he couldn't pick things up yet. It was a formal, department store portrait; the family posed stiffly on individual carpet boxes of varying heights, in front of a drab background, and smiling inanely with dead-eyed grins. There was Michael and his Mother...and Tom.

She was coming up the stairs. He looked around to see if there were any shadows to become one with—but the room was as bright as a surgical theatre, so he quickly found the entrance to the wormhole—no bigger than a pinprick, and thanked Jeffy for his cat-like curiosity before dematerializing into it. She felt a slight chill as she went to retrieve the picture for the police, and noticed it had been moved, ever so slightly...

Then he was there at the scene of the tragedy. He got there early to see the whole thing unfold. There was Tom—just now, hopping off the last step to the dais: anxious as he's confronted by the horde of people stubbornly rooted to their spots in the amorphous queue.

They were unrelenting as Tom squirmed his way to a place in the front—smiling a little at the accomplishment. Also, something completely incongruous appeared amongst the teeming mass of humanity, accompanied by a stench that permeated the whole tunnel. Could none of them smell it? It was the demon Gaap, watching Tom intently as he leaned against the advertising on the back wall. Then suddenly he jerked his head and turned his sights to him, Aleister, breaking the fourth wall of the vision. Gaap's fathomless, black opal eyes brightening a bit on recognizing a copacetic entity. He stood behind Tom, and waved cheekily at Aleister, as he pushed him in front of the train. The action behind Gaap froze, as with a grin that devoured his piranha-like face, he floated on a gust of wind from a train going the other way, through the now petrified crowd, to the place from whence Aleister was watching.

'Aleister...Aleister motherfuck'in Crowley, well I'll be damned. I've been waiting for this moment—you ungrateful prick.'

'Gaap,' Aleister responded dully, and with the look of someone who'd just walked into a fart.

'What can I say, old boy, you'd outgrown your usefulness.'

'After all the shit I did for you,' Gaap whined, like a spurned lover pleading for reconciliation.

'I made a sacrifice to you in thanks for the scarlet woman. Remember that little birdie that flew into my hotel window in Cairo? She did prove useful for the book of the law and my progeny, but in the end, I had to have the poor woman committed. Moreover, as for Willy Yeats, he hated me without your assistance.'

'Yeah, but wiping your ass with my sigil—that was low, man.'

'It is, what it is, my friend. It is, what it is, Aleister said dismissively.

Then as Aleister dusted off his shoulders, Gaap lunged at him, pinning him against a steel support girder with a force that shook shards of rust on to them both.

'I'm gonna eat you to death, motherfucker, he said in a stinky growl that made Aleister puke in his mouth, a little.

'I see you've gone and done it again, haven't you Gaap—bungled another one that is,' Aleister wheezed.

'Whaddya mean? It was a suicide. We get them if it's

suicide,' he said, with a look of astonishment and the labored breathing of a fish being clubbed to death.

'You didn't read his mind before taking him.'

'I didn't have to, he had a note and everything,' he said desperately.

'He changed it, just before you pushed him.'

'But the note said—'

'I wonder what would happen if I informed the Devil of your mistake? Seeing that as a result of another one of your blunders, it'll cost him the annihilation of one of his favorite demons.'

Gaap released him. He didn't want to beg a lowly shadow-being for a lousy break but had to. Anything to avoid the licking he'd get for such a colossal fuck-up.

'Please, Al. Look, I'll let that little stunt with the sigil go if you....forget this ever happened, that we ever saw each other. Catch my drift? However, I'm afraid there's nothing I can do about your little buddy.'

'It's not him I want,' he said.

'Okay, whatever, just forget about the whole thing, kay?'

'Forget what? he said cautiously, and then continued, 'but if I so much as catch the faintest whiff of your—

'You won't, I promise. Catch a needle in the eye,' he said earnestly, crossing himself as he swore the oath. Then the action resumed. Gaap disappeared into the conductor's compartment and Aleister, into the wormhole. He had some business with little Jeffy to attend.

When Tom came to Aleister was gone and so was the alien. Only the old vacuum cleaner salesman remained. The man sat quietly, smoking his cigarette between yellowing fingers, and slurping the swampy coffee, as he read the newspaper with a feigned interest in the flyer section, supposedly admiring the shanks of the pantyhose models while really sussing out Tom's amenability for a chin wag.

It was a leftover reflex from his days as a vagabond Fuller Brush salesman, flogging his sundries to spinsters and widows he'd picked out and followed home from the lineups in grocery and department stores. A sort of profiling-stalking combo that was his bread and butter. He'd gotten into a couple of close scrapes with the law but had the gift of gab, and would charm the pants off the cops and his lonely clientele—throwing in a free gadget for the absentee hubbies.

'I don't know why I bother,' he said nonchalantly—his surefire method of striking up a conversation with a sucker. Tom was still stuck in a fog of depression that had yet to burn off. Each morning was a dawning realization that this was not a recurring dream, but a waking nightmare. He could hear Hubbard's pretentious, British-inflected drawl, pontificating to witless celebs from a back booth-far, far away. The alien was nowhere to be seen. Maybe he'd only crash landed and was somehow able to jerry-rig his ship to get him back to his home planet—but where the hell was Al? Tom's bastion of sanity. His seeming indifference to their circumstances the placebo that staved off the plague of madness he'd taken to calling: the Lonely Town, blues.

Robert Johnson sang like the devil had him by the nuts and was squeezing. A crushed pack of dried Unluckies (he'd recently taken up chain-smoking for want of something better to do) sprinkled tobacco dust on the table. Another cup of joe appeared before him; though the novelty of his host's invisibility had worn off, and caffeine and nicotine was merely the bitter pill he had to swallow to get the night rolling.

Tom had gotten another clue about his past. The neon sign had flashed the substance of the note before the parting signature. He now remembered in its entirety. It was a goodbye memo from his deadbeat dad, who'd left to get a pack of cigarettes and never came back. Forcing his mother to sell the house at a loss, and to scrape by on the wages of a washerwoman, and a government subsidy of food stamps (this much he could recall), while his Dad, tramped around the world, footloose and fancy-free, leaving a string of bastard children in his wake. This was the man sitting before him now, hoping to engage his long lost son in a little conversation. Tom got up and slipped him a shekel. He pitied him the knowledge of his past transgressions and having to come face to face with the consequence of his folly.

'See you around, Pop.'

'See you son. Maybe we can get a drink later.'

'Maybe.'

Tom had already plied the man with whiskey, getting him stewed. In the hope that the libation would lubricate his memory and loosen his lips enough to provide him with some useful information. However, nada. He was nothing but a bullshit artist, and master of trivial details when in his cups, telling Tom things like—'You were a pudgy little kid, but smart as a whip, always with your nose in an encyclopedia, and building models of imaginary cities and stuff.' In short, nothing more than the faded, utterly useless recollections of a low-life, who bugged out on his family. Besides he had an AA meeting to attend. Nice to see you, he'd say. Nice to be seen, the alkys would mutter back.

He didn't like to be late and incur the glowering remonstrations of the alcoholics. He was fastidious about this because tardiness to them was seen as a sure sign of an impending relapse, or at the very least a weakening of one's resolve, as so often happened, when drunks got confronted with the reality of having to live the mundane life of an abstainer. He took his usual fold-out chair in the circle between a hot looking goth chick, and a crusty old priest. He was a hardliner and continuously gave the girl shit for having the temerity to bring up cocaine at a blue card meeting that was supposed to deal exclusively with alcohol addiction. His name was Father Martin. There was no attempt on his part to hide the fact that he was a man of the cloth, as he looked like he lived in his collar, and didn't seem to own a set of civilian clothes.

Tom thought that maybe the good padre was teetering himself, as he always reeked of a lethal-smelling concoction of aftershave, mouthwash, and the faint strains of Fu's Vodka, underlying the whole deception.

The meeting commenced with the chairperson reading the preamble and any other AA-related announcements. This before he or she picked someone at random (in reality one of the chairperson's stooges, who was well-versed in recovery-speak) to open the meeting and commence with what was meant to be an hour-long group therapy session, but always devolved into a chorus of whining and kvetching about the state of their wretched, alcohol-free lives. Before having stumbled upon (literally in some cases), the miracle cure for their alcoholic malady—the not so big book, of Alcoholics Anonymous. Tom was at first grateful to have something besides the old newspaper to read but was ultimately disappointed by what he'd found within the pages of the unassuming book. It opened with a slight autobiography of Bill Wilson: a stiffly written, turgid little tale, styled after a bad Victorian era memoir. The whole thing seemed to hinge on conversion to Christianity for the aspirant to have any hope of successful recovery while insisting that it was a simple, non-denominational philosophy for life. The middle-meat of the manual was great, but the explanation as to how to work the material was incomprehensible and required translation from a sponsor.

The best part was the personal stories, tucked in as an afterthought, in the very back of the book. The meeting itself was like an episode of Tom's favorite TV program. Despite having seen every episode at least fifteen times, he'd watch right along anyway, either too lazy to seek out the remote and change the channel or hoping there'd be a hidden joke in there he'd missed during the last fourteen viewings. At the very least it served as an hour-long respite from the diner, which Tom agreed with Aleister, was a purgatorial weigh station. A checkpoint, somewhere between heaven and hell.

He couldn't help but wonder about the woman who put a ring on it and whether or not to take it off while listening intently to Sonya B. Goode's share. It was supposed to be first names only, but the first stricture broken by members who wanted to be looked up on Facebook. Maybe he could invent a tumultuous history, full of treachery, deceit, and infidelity; a loveless marriage that would warrant what he fantasized about doing with the goth chick, before the blackout. He hadn't taken it further, past the present-moment fantasies—to the physical level, because the toilet stalls were occupied with the likes of Tab and Marilyn living out their post-life fantasies. If he could dream, it would be about fucking her without a care for chivalry, and generosity. Just unabashedly lustful, dirty greediness; not the robotic obligation, that he knew intuitively was the sex act with his wife. It would be the perfect justification for an other-worldly transgression. However, the dull little band still clung to him and was even (annoyingly to her) on the right finger.

It was the first thing Sonya checked for on a prospective lover, and the last thing she looked at before her dreamless-sleep took hold and disintegrated her consciousness. During the smoke break, they'd go off on their own for a flirt and one of their chats, keeping the other men and women with the same ideation as Tom—these thirteen steppers, as they called them in the fellowship at bay, with their singular focus on each other.

'I liked to fuck a lot—plain and simple,' she said,

bluntly, pursing her bee-stung, glossy-black lips, and blowing perfect smoke rings into Tom's face. 'I died while on one of my little misadventures. Death by misadventure is what the coroner ruled it. The dog collar was too tight. You ever tried erotic asphyxiation? The orgasms are like tingle bombs going off in your head. That was the end of my slag-run.'

'Slag-run?' Tom asked with a slight bit of frog in his throat.

'That's what you do when your true love, does something with someone else without your permission or inviting you to join in—behind your back,' she said, spitting a pellet-shaped loogie into the ground. Tom pretended to jingle the shekels in his pocket while re-adjusting his boner.

'You see, I don't think God put us here, Tom. This dimension is a human construct, built with pity and uncertainty. I think we're sent here by people who want this place to exist for their sakes—just in case. People want to be judge and jury—just not the executioner. They're too chicken-shit to push the 'doomed' button, so they wish us here, and then pray for our mortal asses.' Tom smiled and reached out to caress her cheek. She pulled away.

'What are you afraid of Tom—that you're going to run into her?'

'I wouldn't know her to look at her,' he said shyly, to the ground.

'I was a no-good slut to my daddy, but really—just a kickass, take no prisoners feminist, exercising my God-given rights...and talents. So fuck them.'

She licked his face and flicked her cigarette into a puddle, where it sizzled; then strode off, back to the meeting, killing every living thing underfoot. She was a girl who came to the realization—albeit earlier than most, that women were the more powerful of the sexes; that when she wanted to get laid—she could; anytime, anywhere—anyhow. No money? No problem—she need only show up to the party, and the men and women would be on her, for she was the shit.

She especially liked the geeky ones, like Tom. All shy, and awkward, and teachable-like. She'd show them how it's done—how to please her, then pass them on to other, like-minded women. Sonya was good like that.

She had a suicide pact with herself for when the fun of petty sin ran out of steam, even though she knew it was impossible to kill yourself—when you were already dead. The only way to achieve oblivion here was to come up short on the shylock, one too many times like the Dahlia did. The difference was that she would do it deliberately—with style and fury.

Tom took his seat and put up his hand. 'My name's Tom, and I'm an alcoholic.' He proceeded to tell a story that he'd always wanted his life to be. It went something like—that despite having a great but demanding job as an urban planner, and all the money and toys he'd ever dreamt of he was a slave to the demon sauce...

He didn't feel guilty in the slightest. The other members fabricated their life stories, too. Only they'd exaggerate the pitiable aspects, the quantity and lengths they went to, to sustain their addiction. The worse the details, the higher esteem they gained from the group. It was Bizarro world, and had the same ethos - based on the documentaries he'd seen, as prison.

She slid her hand from his crotch to his knee and dug in. He was all hers, just for today.

She'd always been a risk-taker, so after the AA meeting wrapped up—with a group prayer and hug, she dragged him to a church of Satan revival meeting—just for kicks. It was like a Catholic Mass, except the sex, was done out in the open. It was a chancy proposition because if you got caught out in the blackout, they said you'd come to in hell. However, they went, and they fucked right in the open, as did everyone, the entire room a writhing cauldron of wicked ecstasy. They came in unison with the congregation as the high priestess held the chalice aloft, and bellowed, 'Hail Satan!' They left with time to spare. Well before they'd get caught out in the cold and the hellhounds came calling. Sonya decided as she did after every orgasm, that the fun hadn't run out yet, so she'd keep on keeping on.

Tom wanted to hold hands and bask in their mutual clamminess, walking back to the diner together, as a newly consecrated couple. However, instead, when she spotted Bobby K, across the street, and heading toward her favorite shortcut, she called out and dashed to him. Leaving Tom alone, in the atonal wind, and trapped in a dust devil of swirling prop-garbage. He knew then the true nature of her sins, being the latest lust-sick sucker, in a long line of fools to fall prey to her permissive charms. Knowing the score may not have subverted his pangs of anger, self-pity, and guilt, but at least he could say he had her, too, and been promoted to the big club.

He cut through a blind alley that was a different shortcut home (he hated referring to the diner as home, but for now at least, it was) and jumped up to surmount the crumbling wall that lead to his street. He heard a stifled, rattling cough, and saw a disheveled figure—obviously pissed drunk, stumble out from behind a rat infested garbage bin. It shuffled unsteadily toward him, brandishing a teaspoon that—ridiculous as it seemed, was fashioned into a pretty mean-looking weapon, and then fully revealed itself in a slash of moonlight on the wall. In a blink, it was upon him—jamming the prison-style shiv into Tom's pulsating carotid.

'Pop,' he croaked, trying to put a little distance between his throat and the spoons gnarly edge.

'Helluva reveal, eh, kid? Just like in the movies. Can practically hear the the swelling of foreboding music.'

'What the fuck are you doing?'
Tom's Dad had that dead-set, haunted and desperate look, like the Dahlia's, in his booze-soaked eyes.

'I've always been no-good, son: no-good husband, no-good father, and no-good with money. The shylock's after me, so be a good boy and hand over the shekels. No matter what happens, you're going to a good place—me, I think not, eh? Hand it over—now!'

Tom spat in his face; a great big fluorescent booger that made a smacking sound as it hit Pop's bulbous nose, and swung languidly back and forth before dropping off with a splat.

'You vile fuck. Rot in hell!'

Tom's Dad flashed his teeth and pressed the spoon harder to his throat, threatening to pop the bulging vein.

'I'll cut you, kid. I'll cut you real good, and slow-like.'

Just as he began to saw Tom's neck, something exploded from Pop's chest, spattering blood on Tom's glasses and into his gaping mouth. It was a giant set of claws, cleaving Pop's, still-quivering heart. It looked black and diseased, contrasted with the forepaw in the fluorescent moon-shade.

Pop sucked at the cold night, puffing desperately like he smoked his cigarettes, trying to catch a breath, then expelled one last shallow whiff of mist from his nostrils, before collapsing in stages to reveal a hulking wolf, rising up slowly and deliberately to its full bi-pedal height. It loomed over them as it held the bloated heart to its jaws, then sucked out the internal vena cava and its inferior, quaffing the last of the juice from the deflated muscle, and tossed the skin to the side.

'Gotta a smoke, kid?' It asked casually. 'I always like to have a smoke while I'm eating...and chewing gum.'
Tom fumbled around in his pocket and handed over the whole pack, dropping the lighter. He daren't pick it up. The wolf did, lit it, and inhaled deeply, bloodying the end.

Tom, remembered, too late now, the repeated warnings of Aleister to never walk alone. That everyone was as desperate as the next. Even blood-kin would cut your throat to keep the wolves at bay.

'Where are the others,' Tom asked while trying to squint enough light into the darkness to see the rest of them.

'Don't worry. I'm all by my lonesome. Somebody must be thinking about you.'

'How do you know?' He asked. My wife, maybe? What's she like? Is she pretty? All the questions someone in the dark would want to know about their mystery spouse. As much trepidation as excitement, like a curious groom, before an arranged marriage.

'You're getting a bit too chummy with, Aleister.'

'Yeah, so what, he's my friend,' Tom said, assuredly.

The wolf shook its head, flicking blood and drool from its jowls. 'Listen kid, he ain't nobody's friend.'

Tom looked perplexed and vulnerable, as he gazed up at the wolf. He wanted the conversation to proceed along the lines of complete mundanity. Like the ones around the espresso machine at work, where he'd insert a Cagney or Bogart, and the conversation would die instantly. That didn't involve topics like after death experiences, magic, giant people-eating ravens, and acts of bestiality amongst talking wolves. Fat chance, he thought, and was waiting for Rod Serling to emerge from around the corner to endorse filterless cigarettes before introducing the exciting conclusion.

'He's after your son. Needs him for some magic ritual, The Great Operation, he called it. He's dead meat if Aleister gets a-hold of him.'

This revelation, said matter of factly, firstly that he had a son, and that his child was in danger, put a full-stop to his questions. His eyes lit up, as if gifted with something glowing and pulsating.

The wolf continued. 'Aleister's found a wormhole.'

'A wormhole?'

It sucked and picked at its incisors. 'I ain't got time to give you a lesson in Quantum Physics, kid. I only know what Aleister told me. I can hardly understand it myself. I mean, look at this situation. The whole thing is loony-tunes. He could only give me the version for trollops, he says. He got summoned by one of your son's buddies with a ouija board. It caused a tear in the space-time, thing-a-ma-jig. Took forever for him to get the call. He's not as infamous as he once was. It lets him go back in time—right up to the present, but no further. It's a porthole, a doorway to every dimension. Right now, he's only a shadow of his former self, can't do anything but spook people. He needs—get this, a human sacrifice to become fully embodied. He'll do it, too. He's ruthless. Son-of-a-bitch promised to take me with him. Serves me right. As it was in life, so it was here. Bottom-line is, you gotta get outta here, or your son's a goner.'

Tom grabbed two fistfuls of its soft underbelly and strained to pull it toward him. 'How? Tell me, how the fuck do I get out of here?'

'I dunno,' it said resignedly, as it got down on all

fours.

'Maybe hitch a ride with Aleister,' it said, as it pawed at the pocket of Pop's jacket, jingling the pile of coins inside.

'Son-of-a-bitch,' Tom said.

'He promised to take me for a ride once, back in the days when he said he fancied me...
But remember, you'll only be ectoplasm, and not able to interact with matter enough to make a difference. Only watch, quiet as a stowaway in the cargo hold. It would take some of the truly evil shit—a spell of necromancy for you to intercede on your son's behalf. Just don't let him catch you or he'll cast you out—to oblivion.'

For fuck's sake, okay, I'll...I'll figure it out. How's Dahlia doing?' Is she okay?

The wolf snickered. 'They wanted Marilyn all along, Tom. All my babies turned out wonky. As above so below. Probably because of all those back-alley abortions.

'Thanks,' Tom said, and then with genuine sympathy, I'm sorry you...Look, I got a shitload of shekels now. I'll give you whatever you need. Aleister said you could buy anything here,' he said, stooping slightly to her eye level. She spun around to leave. 'Where are you gonna go?'

'To oblivion. You can buy time, Tom, but not an emanation of your humanity.'

'Wait. I want to help you.'

'Even the God's die, like dogs—alone,' the wolf called back, as it trotted around the corner.

Tom stepped over the cadaver and left it as food for the rats, who were becoming more aggressive in their approach of the body with the coppery scent of gory death beginning to permeate the alley. He wondered if they could talk like the wolves. 'I'm just leaving guys, have at her.' 'Fuck off, then,' one of them spat, as it darted toward the face and worked at the nose, tearing off the bulbous tip, and took the Egyptian route to the brain.

Desperation and betrayal were the keywords in the unwritten mission statement of Lonesome Town, he reflected; watching with disgusted fascination, the rats take care of the bulk of the maggot's work. If his father was willing to cut his son's throat to gain a little more time here what was Aleister, his surrogate capable of? Even though he'd had the displeasure of meeting his biological father in the flesh, his mother, though her memory, not a very clear picture—even now, resounded within him, because her legacy came from his heart's memory.

Everyone he'd met thus far seemed to be living for residual drives. Things that had been left unfulfilled or unfinished. Had his life been about something more significant than simply getting by? Did he have some desire or dream that propelled him through life and whatever this was? Nothing was showing up here. The scant memories his father had provided him with indicated there wasn't much left to discover.

He caught a glimpse of himself in a derelict storefront window; racking the focus of his eyes to render the blown-up mannequins blurry, and himself in high-definition, taking a thorough inventory of his physical characteristics. Not a corner of the eye glance—before going into the office assay. This time, a thorough inspection from the top of his barbered head, his nondescript face, brown suit, down to the plastic-looking, supermarket loafers, on his tiny feet. The total added up the lame-duck winnings from a penny ante, poker game—bupkis. He decided to press his luck with the blackout and take a detour to the Shylock's place of business.

They said it was easy to find—an old rooming house turned den of iniquity, on the other side of the tracks. Railway employees once used it as a flophouse between cross-country trips. On the whole, they had been a pretty degenerate bunch; frittering away their hard-earned wages, drinking, gambling, and fighting—mostly amongst themselves. Now the tenants were transients, looking for a place to fix, fuck, or die trying. He knew he was a fool, going on his own—unarmed; but he needed to buy a couple more seconds of consciousness to follow Aleister and sneak into the wormhole with him. Then convince or coerce him to take him to his son.

The door was innocuous looking, but on trying the handle-bar—steel reinforced, with a sliding slot for speedy deposits, pleading one's case for access into the inner sanctum, or in Tom's case, an audience with the Shylock. He was granted permission when he name-dropped Aleister and pushed past art-like installations of human degradation. The first floor, occupied solely by junkies, was spartan but for the waning candlelight and fetid bodies of nodding somnambulists, strewn about the shooting gallery. It was apparent they'd forgone a wash for fear, Tom heard, that the potency of the drug would be diminished and therefore made everyone who came within their vicinity pay the price for their addiction. The crackers and scabby meth-heads were everywhere, skittering about the ground like sketchy cockroaches, hoovering up popcorn that they'd mistaken for rock, and pissing everyone off in general. Every other transaction was conducted behind closed doors.

He of was escorted into a dimly lit back room, before a broad woman spilling from the seams of her silk kimono, plopped behind a distressed oak desk, smoking a cigarette from a long, yellowing ivory holder.

Tom spoke first, haltingly. 'I'm here to see...the Shylock.'

'You got something for me, kid?'

Tom brought his Dad's booty out of his pocket and dangled the little leather bag from his finger. 'I need something that maybe, you don't sell. I gotta ask, why shekels? Why not dollars or pounds?

Her clownishly made-up face, like a sweaty pig with

a broad stroke of lipstick, disappeared for a minute, until the smoke from her exhalation dissipated, then: 'Cause it's my people's money, and pounds are what I gotta' lose—a few anyway,' she snorted. 'We sell everything, for a price.' She rolled out from behind the desk in an ancient wheelchair, and parked herself with the stirrups jammed against his shins.

'I want to buy some time.'

'I hate to break it to you, but you got nothing but time. So why the hell would you want to pay for more when you got an eternal supply for free?'

He cleared his throat. 'I need a few minutes more consciousness…before the blackout.'

She looked right through him, to the shadow behind him, who'd been his escort through his preview of hell. He felt it acknowledge her thoughts, and depart through the back wall.

She took another long drag that consumed the other half of her cigarette and spoke quietly through the smoke.

'I don't want anyone to get any bright ideas—everybody works for somebody else, and somebody wants everybody's job, if you catch my drift. Don't want to end up like the Dahlia. She was one of my girls for a while, good earner, too, till Al, good samaritan that he is, bought out her contract. Damn-fool didn't know what he was getting himself into so—cut her loose. Left her to her own vices and she took care of herself. I know what you're up to.

Tom cleared his throat and crossed his arms, though he knew this was a 'tell' in poker.

'The only guy that ever cracked it was that scientist, the one with the electronic warning voice in the wheelchair.' Tom knew him. Everybody on the planet did.

'He tried to pull the same stunt, and you know where he ended up? In oblivion. Do you know where that is? Nowhere—no place, nothing, donesky, that's where. Do you want to know what it is?

Tom gulped and nodded, guiltily, he did.

'The sleep of the dead, erased, like you never existed. The guy was an atheist, so probably feels right at home, but still.

'How do you know...that's where he is?'

'Cause we're the only ones know he ever existed. Shame, all them big brains wasted.'

'You aren't as smart as he was, or famous even.

Nobody's beating down your door to have you show up as a guest at their seance, so what makes you think you can pull it off?'

'Because I never did have anything to lose,' he said and didn't flinch, as she exploded in hacking laughter.

'You know what you are, kid? You're a real mensch—that's your superpower— likeability. You remind me of Jimmy Stewart. An affable everyman. That's real power.'

He already knew that, somehow. Knew that his mother had comforted him with this fact when Tom had been inevitably relegated to the friend-zone with prospective girlfriends—gotten him picked for the best recess baseball team, though he warmed the bench and was voted most inspirational. The thing that had allowed him to slide-by in school, from kindergarten through college, and all the way up to the middle of every job. The consideration that led him to settle on the used, reliable, economy-model for his wife. 'You could get away with bloody murder if you had the heart,' she said, rolling back to her desk. 'I like you, and I don't like nobody, except myself, when I take a selfie from a great height. So, here's the deal: you give me all you got, save for one, just in case.'

He spilled the contents of the velvet bag onto the desk, and dug out the strays, cascading them over the others. They were slugs. All but one. Crude counterfeit coins, fashioned from the backs of appliances.

She picked up the single shekel, stared at it intently, then placed it in a drawer, beside two others. 'Now you got no choice. You leave tonight,' she said, with a wink. 'But remember, everybody, knows'...

'Knows what?' He said.

'Everything.

Chapter 7

Tom watched in awe as Hubbard expounded on the most recent expansion to his science of the mind, he now called, Scientology, spraying spittle on his captive audience as he enunciated the science and droned the 'ology.' However, lost Tom and the others at the part of the origin myth where Gorgon, the intergalactic overlord, deposited his essence in a mountain somewhere in Wenatchee, and was right now, as he spoke, unleashing them upon the earth. Tom couldn't help but imagine Gorgon's sperm-monster army contrasted with his squad of dead soldiers, and wondered how they were faring, storming Sonya's foxhole. Then Hubbard's viscous baritone disintegrated his reverie like one of the phasers in Star Trek—'To take over the minds of ignoramus assholes like yourselves, who haven't bought my course to go clear yet.' It was a ripping yarn—well told with a mouthful of smoke and snot. Then Tom thought—I better be discreet; try not to think about wormholes, and think about Sonya's instead. Right about now Pop—if he wasn't having his head gnawed by the guy buried up to his neck behind him—would be jocular from the drink and shooting the shit with the boys, nothing but a pathetic blowhard, working them like he did the lonely house fraus who were good for a useless gadget or two. It made him love his mother even more, though it was blind faith in the idea of her that resonated in every atom of his discarnate body. Aleister was there too, in spritus, and strangely silent, staring into his coffee, and stirring it with the repetitive motion of a baker's mixer, ending with a ting, and starting again. Then devoured the biggest piece of apple pie that Tom, had ever seen—perhaps fortifying himself for one of his long, strange trips, while everyone else was comatose. Another thing Tom noticed, he was fading from the picture like a polaroid in reverse.

Martin liked to have a smoke and a nip of the good stuff he stashed behind a stack of cowboy novels in his desk cupboard, Sunday afternoons, after mass. On one such lazy day, meant to be one of prayer and reflection, while pacing the garden path, he noticed fresh earth piled atop one of the neglected flower beds. He checked to make sure he wasn't being watched (as Kilty had an uncanny knack for popping up out of thin air), then knelt to examine what looked like one of the coyote's tunnels in the Road-Runner cartoons. It was a shit concealment. He'd seen this kind of thing before back in his copper days; it would've been used as a repository for bodies, booty from a heist, or cash, but was now the preferred means of disposal for incriminating evidence of a far more degenerate kind: photographs, magazines—hard drives—fag-paedo smut.

He wanted Kilty bad, like the drink that was calling to him from behind Louis L'amour but had come up short when it came to the hard-evidence he required to justify filing a formal complaint to the Bishop. Overall creepiness, gossip and gut feelings wouldn't cut it, and Martin's report—vigorously and passionately two-finger typed, inevitably disregarded like his final notices and junk mail, or end up buried like its predecessors in deep, bureaucratic graves. He cleared the aerated mound, then dug like a desperate gopher, stopping to check again for prying eyes from Kilty's bedroom window. For a second, he thought he saw a silhouette staring at him from behind the crack in the jaundiced-looking curtains, but blinked the apparition away, and continued, his fingers finally clawing at something plastic, hollow sounding for something so big...and rectangular—it was a black box—the missing hard drive from Kilty's computer. I got you, cocksucker, he hissed as he squished the dirt into an object that resembled his long lost brass knuckles.

It was just about dinner time so he remade the hill exactly how he'd found it, and started to formulate a plan to exhume the evidence later that night when Kilty would be ending his evening with what he assumed was a noisy wank. From then on he did everything by the book—his book—his rules.

He cashed in a favor from his one remaining buddy

on the force, twiddling away his last shifts before retirement behind a desk, who'd jump at the chance to get involved in something juicy. They went over the contents in the evidence room, away from anyone who might want the controversial-type collar for themselves. Martin heaved at what he saw: hazy, jittery, handheld footage, of the boys, doing truly satanic things. Lewd and lascivious (the legalese used to describe his entrapment at the hands of that dirty little whore), forbidden carnal acts on a besotted Kilty, who seemed to smile smugly at Martin from behind the screen, and in retrospect, every night from his cell next door—the makeshift set for his felonious productions.

They sequestered the hard drive—unlabelled, in the very back of the cage; hidden behind a tangle of bikes and other crap. Martin was going to do it by the book alright; tappity-tap-tap the fucking report, mail it, third class, then—unleash hell.

Satan was too busy funnin' with them yokels to give a shit about Gaap's latest blunder. Yeah, it had cost him a demon; however, it was only one of the scented ones, an aid in successful aromatherapy, or some other such new-age nonsense.

Besides, he was right in the middle of perpetrating his civic duties when he decided to tune back into the fact, starting with his first-ever town hall meeting. Just now, jive talking about getting some nukes to blow up the neighboring county if they didn't hush up about the sewage Gristle was dumping in one of the pristine rivers that cut through the state. When one of the council members had the nerve to oppose Satan's motion to arm themselves to the teeth and blow them to kingdom come, he turned himself into an animated leviathan, worthy of one of the classic Disney films—incinerating the offending naysayer with a white-hot torch of realistic looking fire. All the while marveling at the contrast between his cartoon self, and the live-action uproar at the meeting.

Word eventually got back to the White House, that little-old Gristle, had acquired nuclear arsenal enough, to wipe out a whole-half of the United States, and was threatening to do so, if anyone fucked with them.

The Donald's hands were sometimes handcuffed but rarely idle. Therefore any deeds done with said digits were impervious to the devil's work. He was a multi-tasker, who could pleasure himself behind the oval office desk, finger through an amendment to the constitution, during a meeting with his foreign affairs minister, while advancing over the curves of the former Miss Universe he'd hired as his new, Secretary of State. Therefore too busy to contemplate the problems of a piss-ant county, like Gristle. She: sipping a crystal magnum of champagne, perched atop the console with her long legs spread, while The President's fingers hovered somewhere between her newly discovered g-spot, and the shiny-red, doomsday button. Moreover, until he returned to the subject of the great wall of America, and reneged on his promise to have Mexico fund its construction, the country believed that the only devil they had to contend with was the biblical one.

Aleister left behind a little piece of himself with Jeffy, the day he was summoned by the kids to the shack. They would be the knights in his gambit to engage with his guardian angel: vital to his success, but ultimately dispensable, as in any game of chess. He left just enough residual energy behind to generate voices in Jeffy's head. Entreaties from a vacant hemisphere in his brain that compelled him to do evil things, like light fires, torture animals, wet the bed, and Aleister's bidding. He had to be flesh and blood—fully human once again, to engage with magic. For this, he required the sacrifice of one in his honor. For unbelievable as it seems, humans occupy a much higher station in the spiritual hierarchy than ghosts (and can attain the level of demigod), who are only powerful in their menial task of scaring people, and then only if their victims allow their fear—based on ignorance, to get the best of them. If they knew their potential, they would swat these dark emanations away like pesky flies.

He encouraged Jeffy, to practice on inferior species before the much more challenging task of sacrificing an actual, live, in the flesh, 1.5 gallons of blood, homosapien. As for the lamb, very few virgins still existed in the world, even in the realm of supposedly innocent, twelve, and thirteen-year-olds. Heeding Aleister's advice, Jeffy conveniently started with birds. One day, while hidden from view behind the woodpile and armed with a steak knife, he waited patiently for a baby robin to come down from the tree, and peck for worms on the freshly mowed lawn. Esmeralda's familiar, a hairless Manx, caught wind of Jeffy's plan, from another familiar, who lived down the road. The Manx thought he'd do Jeff a solid, knowing cats were next on his list, and so swept in, and caught the robin for him; toying with it first, before depositing the mangled birdy, at Jeff's feet. So he skipped cats and went right to dogs.

Michael was listless. Not because of the voices (the loudest being a demon named Gaap), but because of Kilty's insistence that they consummate their relationship before Michael was released from his obligations as his concubine. The thought made him turn entirely inward, to the deep well within his brain that he retreated to, whenever Kilty's perverted desire got the best of him. He was now a shell of his former radiant self: a wane, defeated-little boy. When Jeff, suggested that he was going to up the ante a bit with the sacrifice of his neighbor's dog, and could use his help, Michael, agreed to be his assistant—compliant as the living dead. Jeff didn't tell him about the pact he'd made with Aleister, that soon, Michael, would be usurped as the most popular seventh-grader in the world, and he, king Jeff, would control all the marbles, and cuties, and candy, literally.

Blue was a lovely old dog: he was half-blind, had a bucked-off tail, and a bum leg, but a real pleasant disposition. He always licked Jeff when he gave it a treat and cowered a little when he patted him on the head. Jeff and Michael led the dog by its rope—to the shed. He made no fuss. They couldn't poison it as there had to be bloodshed: Aleister's orders. Michael held him down, and Blue gave them one last forlorn look before it was over. Michael watched the whole thing from outside of his body. Disgusted and ashamed, but too weak to protest, or put a stop to this soul-destroying crime. Jeff's machete did the deed quickly, with only a whimper and a couple of quivers as the life drained from its body. The blood gushed over the board, pooling in the recesses of the letters and numbers, as with a sucking sound, like a fat kid vacuuming up the last of the milkshake foam at the bottom of the glass. The Ouija licked itself clean.

The last of their bright, childish lights, went out that moment, for good.

Aleister manifested from the shadows, appearing to them as a faded, flickering, ghost-like projection, on the clapboard wall. The rays of sunlight that cut through the cracks and perforated his image made it look as if he was imprisoned in a claustrophobic cell. He looked inconsolate too, as if Jeff had betrayed him in some way. His eyes bore into him with an expression sure to crush any child's heart—supreme disappointment. Jeff's instincts were no longer his own (hence the sudden outbursts of frenzied masturbation at the dinner table) but obeyed them faithfully; his reaction time to the voices was fly-like in speed as if always anticipating an incoming swatter.

Jeff swept Michael into his dangly, orangutan-like arms, and pressed the bloodied edge of his freshly christened weapon to Michael's creamy-white neck. Instantly, Michael had a notion why he had chosen to befriend the lumbering giant rather than cower, head in his locker, like the other kids when Jeff's shadow passed over them in the school hall. It was to keep a potential conqueror close. Closer than the kids' his mom and teachers expected him to hang around with, so Jeff became the 'golden boy's' protector, turned assassin.

Jeff looked to Aleister for approval—for a glimmer: a hint or twinge, to indicate he was doing the righteous thing—a when, and if to proceed.

Aleister responded, in a tinny-sounding voice, like the

scratchy playback of an Edison dictating machine, and pronounced: 'He is not a virgin.'

'He sure as hell is,' Jeff, said, loosening his grip for a moment, indignant at the suggestion that his intel was faulty and Michael had beaten him to Elaine.

Michael dropped like a dead-weight out of Jeff's hold, spun around, and plunged the knife into Jeff's chest. He watched for a moment as Jeff staggered to the table and in perfect, climactic death-scene fashion, collapsed onto the board. Michael tried to play the part of the escaped hero, by kicking open the door, but it stood fast—solid as a brick wall. The camp lanterns rattled and hissed, toppling to the floor: shooting kerosene trails of blue fire to the four corners of the tinder-dry shack. Michael looked to the one broken-out window to flee from, but Aleister's madly-flickering apparition floated over to it and stood in his way; beckoning the boy, to dare approach him. He wasn't sure if Aleister had achieved full actualization, or was still in a lesser, hence weaker Astral-form, but knew he'd have to take a chance at the window or burn to death for his cowardice.

'Fuck it,' he said and flung himself through the apparition, and out the window.

As he passed through the dense, fog-like ghost, he felt a white-hot terror, that incinerated what he knew to be a part of his very soul. Tom, his stepfather, had lied to him when he told him not to be afraid of the ghosties and ghoulies under his bed, assuring him that they were harmless and couldn't hurt him. They could all right, he thought, just in places that couldn't be seen.

Chapter 8

Tom closed his eyes as if the big sleep had taken him like the others, but was watching intently through the narrowest of slits in his scrunched eyelids and crusty lashes. It was the first time he'd been conscious during the blackout, and he wondered if anything out of the ordinary happened while they were in the induced coma. He saw a glowing, Bouguereau-worthy, angel cupping its hands and peering in. He waved at it, but it hissed and turned demonic as it flew off on realizing Tom had spotted it.

When Aleister was satisfied everyone was out-cold, he slipped out of the booth and disappeared from Tom's view, but he could hear the distinct creak of the toilet door and knew this was where Aleister kept hid the entrance to the wormhole.

Aleister got into one of the stalls and was surprised to find Norma Jean slumped over the toilet. He sat her up and briefly contemplated taking the sleeping beauty with him for a little fun in the snow. Her lifeless body was tempting but knew her dumb-blonde routine would grate, so let her body flop, and slipped into the unoccupied one, next.

Tom tiptoed to the little boys but stopped to take a quick look around the place to see what it looked like while everyone was sleeping. Nothing out of the ordinary, really, he thought. Just a rundown diner packed with loudly snoring celebrity customers and confirmation that they drooled, farted and muttered in their sleep as he did, and was tempted to leave a note for Tab to check his silk boxers. But then thought, Nah, life is better for its little surprises. He pushed the door gently, grimacing as if to minimize the long, drawn-out squeak, and went inside. At first, all he could hear in the pitch black was the echoing drip of the leaky faucet but then: the unbuckling of a belt, trousers falling to the floor, the sharp report of a toilet seat, fart burst, and a genuine sigh of relief. He continued toward the sounds; crushing a sodden toilet roll underfoot, and splashing what he hoped was a puddle of water until finally, the tip of his nose bumped into one of the stall doors, and he (waiting for the cover of still more flatulence), pushed his way inside.

Aleister snapped open a bejeweled box. It had once been the crypt for the ruby ring he'd gifted his wife, Rose, his one and only scarlet woman, to celebrate her contribution in Egypt to his life's most celebrated work thus far: *The Book of The Law.* He didn't want to part with it, not under any circumstances, but he'd failed to pay off his opium tab (the Chinaman also ran an opium den and a laundry in the basement of the restaurant) and his vigorish for protection to the Shylock. So it was the precious keepsake or banishment to Oblivion, and reluctantly decided it was the ring that had to go. The Shylock wore it proudly on her fat-little pinky finger. She never failed to display her hand when Aleister would show up to pay her extortionate interest. The Chinaman thought he was reimbursed fully with the bestowment by Aleister of the power of invisibility but was just a case of over-familiarity. For he never left the confines of the restaurant and preferred hiring his fellow countrymen to Westerners, as it gave an air of authenticity to his brand of American-style, Chinese cuisine. So while at the restaurant, he was practically invisible and only realized the fraud when it was pointed out to him while practicing nude Tai-Chi in the middle of the busy restaurant.

The wickedest man in the world, actually felt a slight twinge of sentimentality as he cracked open the box, and a light began to emanate from tiny perforations in the crushed velvet. However, swiftly, before this feeling could take hold and compromise his decision making on the mission, he deliberately ruined the sentiment with another burst of sweet and sour wind.

Tom heaved himself up to peer over the wall of the stall to see a little vortex, the size of a carnival lollipop, manifest from the box. As the orb grew it became a swirling funnel of kaleidoscopic colors, and then hovering before Aleister—the wormhole having attained the size of a basketball, grabbed it by the rubbery sides, and tore it open: shaping the newly formed opening into a picture window, replete with a stunning view of a wild and snowy mountain tundra. A smiley Shirpa waved and beckoned for the still enthroned Aleister, to join him. He shook back and indicating just a moment with his index finger, sheepishly pulled up his pants, and stepped through the rippling frame. Immediately the portholes parameters began to shrink, making a loud sucking sound as it did so, like partially obstructed water draining from a sink. With one last heave, Tom threw himself over and dove in, after him, softly disappearing into a powdery snowbank on the other side. He cleared some of the crystalline flakes from his lenses and watched the window close; the sphere contracting in an ever smaller circle to inevitable black; like the fade-out at the end of silent movies. Then they were gone.

Make no bones about it; Martin was no angel. Nor was he delusional enough to think he'd ever be nominated for posthumous canonization. Posterity was for phonies, whose motivation was purely selfish, and legacy in his mind was the successful perpetration of bullshit on an ignorant populace. His records, both as a cop and a priest were spotty, to put it kindly. Both blemished by bouts of alcoholism, and the consequence of his actions while under the influence of booze and the attendant grandiosity. The stress from covering up his violations of policy and procedure had caused a chain-smoking habit that brought a nasty case of chronic obstructive pulmonary disease to go along with it.

His days as a beat cop looked like something out of the movie, *Serpico*, except he wasn't the good looking hero battling corruption, he was one of the dirty ones, and looked more like Tommy Lee Jones, if his face had been put through a meat grinder again. He was the ringleader of the recipients of kickbacks: proceeds from the little protection racket he ran from within the force—just tips really, for out-muscling the muscle of organized crime, and administered the occasional discretionary beating to thugs who terrorized the excellent, white—hardworking, blue-collar, constituents living in his territory.

A minor indiscretion with a minor had ended his marriage, and left the children bastards and made a bastard out of him. It brought his shady career to an equally inglorious end, with the not so subtle suggestion that he take early retirement to avoid the shame of being fired and bringing that same disgrace, and a possible investigation, to the already compromised force. The shit was running upward, past the little molehill he'd built for himself within the castle, straight to the district attorney's office.

He heeded their advice and skulked off, collecting his modest pension, amassed throughout his 'colorful' career and became a priest.

He may have been a son-of-a-bitch, but at least he wasn't a paedo, like that faggot Kilty, he justified. Not with cunning and forethought. Not on purpose. She said she was eighteen. Yeah, her ID was a little sketchy, an obvious forgery more like it, but her body would've gotten a castrated saint convicted of lewd and lascivious battery.

He thought he might've killed one once. A suspected kiddie fiddler, that is, but couldn't be sure. Said the creep was messing with one of the local businessman's daughters, so for the right price, he meted out justice. Only this time he'd been a little too hard on the kid. Moreover, there was the lingering question as to whether the kid had been guilty at all—that they were boyfriend and jilted girlfriend—Lord knows they started young these days. Maybe Martin had been manipulated into doing the dirty work for her. Who knew. He didn't follow-up with the hospital; it was too risky with the heat already on him something fierce.

Martin was good at doctoring reports. He'd had to be, firstly to cover his own ass, but also to implicate suspects that might've gotten off on some measly technicality.

Kilty was out past his curfew again, so Martin thought he had enough on him to get him temporarily put out to pasture—but that's all they'd do. Hide him from the law and justice in some mountaintop monastery for therapy and retraining. However, before Kilty disappeared into exile, he wanted to put the screws to him first. He'd rough him up a little, in subtle places that he knew. Break a few of his smaller, unnecessary bones, then parade him in front of the parishioners, and, like Pontius Pilate, ask them what they wanted him to do with him. He'd seen some pretty hairy shit go down in the Burroughs when an unruly crowd went mob and took justice into their own hands. They'd defrock Martin for it—but so what? There was a good trade in the P.I business for ex-cops, and he'd finally be like the lovably roguish heroes in Chandler stories he'd always aspired to emulate.

He poured himself another scotch, aged to perfection—barely legal guys, he'd joke, when bartending for his cronies, and lit a cigarette. He missed the sound a typewriter made as he'd punch the keys and they'd pummel the paper. Now it sounded like he was playing the piano on a practice-pad, with cotton balls taped to his fingertips.

He wondered how he was going to resist the temptation to kill him. To beat him into a paste that crime scene cleanup would have to scrape off the floor, and remembered the righteousness he'd feel bringing this toilet scum to justice. The type of sentence the system should impose on them: the family given five minutes alone with the creep, to do with them as they wilt, that was the whole of Martin's law.

It was the glory that eluded him for the entirety of his policing career because he'd never done anything on the up and up. He'd always taken shortcuts, and the back door to get the job done, and hence allow others to take credit for his work, or take the blame for their failings like a vigilante.

He took a pull from the bottle this time, almost missing his lips—cause that's what they're made for—and waited for the sound of Kilty's footfall on the steps.

He thought the drink calmed him, allowed him to see more clearly, and lowered his inhibitions in a way that made him act decisively, without dithering. That he even drove better, with more confidence when he'd had a few. Things only went south when he was forced to collaborate with others. They were the ones who fucked up, who'd pussy-out when the work became hard and dirty. His ex-wife would attempt to impart insight during his nightly rehash of another day's bitter disappointment: tell him that he was nothing but a pathetic, broken down, impotent old loser and that if he could only see past his swollen and veiny red nose—slow down to see the dead trees for the scorched earth...Goddamnit, Martin, she'd scream, please have a moment of clarity, parroting his human resources-mandated sponsor. If he'd stop replaying in lurid, porn-like detail over and over again, the loop of pain and anguish, he refused to fast forward past, to better times ahead, that he could if he wanted, come clean, hit reset and start fresh with the new day instead of crawling to bed at the crack of dawn. That was the reason for the career change he told himself over and over again. However, to him, that was a bunch of hocus-pocus. Magical thinking that the headshrinkers sent you on your way with after your hour was up. So he would have another, and vent his frustrations, real and imagined, on the nearest and dearest, the most vulnerable persons in his vicinity: the ones he loved most. For not loving the shit in his head away, and their failure to do so turned love into mutual hatred, and their tolerance into revulsion.

When he drank, there was no distinction between the two. The most vivid, reoccurring flashback, was when he was beaten to a pulp by his crew. The officers he ran the little side business with, who found out that he was double-dipping: a dirty cop and a snitch for the feds to boot—a rat's move to save his own skin.

He swore he could hear moaning coming from Kilty's room. Knew it to be so, and had another drink. Martin was pounding them back so fast now, that he denied himself the pleasures of the slow-burn sensation, and effervescent calm as it trickled down his throat, and into his molten gullet. Skipping right over the rush of contentment, and Zen-like peace, that was owed him—to the rage. He was a fucking volcano, man. His head was the peek and his insides the seething—combustible contents, ready to blow. The night and his report were progressing at a turgid, dirge-like pace, with the tap-tap of the keyboard, the moaning next door, and his infernal voice egging him on. Fuck the paperwork and fuck subjecting himself to the bureaucrats and their bullshit, then waiting like a mug for it to snail its way into the hands of someone who gave a shit and could make a difference. That's why he took matters into his own hands. Fuck waiting for God; he was going to sort this one out.

He crept down the hall, armed with only his curled, bloodless fists, and the resolve to reduce Kilty to a smear on the carpet. Something inside stirred, as if disturbed in the commission of something genuinely sinful. Martin braced himself against the wall, and with a swift kick to the sweet spot; obliterated the press-board door.

There, little Michael, the golden boy of the parish, the smartest and prettiest of all the angels with dirty faces, stood naked and trembling before him. A trickle of blood running down his inner thigh—while Kilty smiled with the smugness of a pimp who'd just reestablished his dominance over a wayward whore. He was luxuriating in the unholy mess he'd made of the bed and casually smoked a cigarette. The boy ran to Martin, wrapping himself around his paunchy midriff, and collapsed to his knees, his body wracked with sobs.

Martin implored God to bless him and keep him faithful to the spirit he had given him.

Kilty seemed to relish the beating Martin was administering him. He thought himself spent after he'd finished with Michael, but was experiencing a resurgence of arousal that shocked him. He thought Martin lacked the grace of a professional pugilist of love, but Martin, as a result of his short stature, always fought from a place of fear that made him angrier still, and served to fuel his desperation, thus giving him what former opponents called 'heart' and a puncher's chance, thus effective for Kilty's ends.

He was beyond rage now. He'd transcended to a state that could only be classed by color. He was red. Crimson with hatred and loathing for the old saggy body that he was throttling beyond eventual identification. It would take the teeth—embedded in the carpet after he was through with him. With each blow years of anger turned—inward, were shed from him, and he felt his soul cleansed—exorcized of its tainted aspect. There would be no mercy or discretion. He did not care to whom the assault might be reported or the consequences—all time was here and now. He was unhinged.

Then Kilty began to twitter, ever so slightly, spraying gore and teeth over the sheets. He'd gone to heaven for a moment on masochistic pleasure-wings, but spat at its tepid perfection, and was cast back down to the blessed earth and all its carnal glory. Having been reduced to nothing more than a heaving pulp, he splayed his broken fingers and cast Martin from him. Conjuring an invisible force that catapulted him across the room, and stuck him, shit-like, to the wall.

'Thank you for that, my friend,' he sputtered, to the paralytic Martin. 'The last time I received a beating of that quality was some time ago, and cost me a fortune.'

'Now Michael, go and get the others, I will need a hand with getting Martin and myself down to the temple.'

Martin couldn't move his face, but watched from the corner of his eye; the now calm and composed child dressed and left Kilty and him alone.

Kilty rolled his broken body off the bed, and onto the

floor. The sheets stuck to him, costuming him like a Caesar as he pulled himself up and into his desk chair. Kilty raised his arm and spread his fore and index fingers. Martin winced, as he felt his arms and legs rend from their sockets.

'I could easily draw and quarter you with a nod of my head, or rip your head off by clearing the sleep from my eyes, but alas, I need you alive. It wouldn't be a true sacrifice if you were already dead, and much less efficacious—a lowly offering, like one of Renfield's rats to Dracula.'

Martin tried to respond, but his jaw locked with tetanus.

'You are about to bear witness to a great happening—something the average punter will never see: the transmigration of souls. Mine to Michael's body, and his...kicked to the curb, if you will. A gift to the dreamless sleeper: the Goddess Oblivion.' Martin could hear them now, marching and clamoring for him up the stairs.

He prayed for divine intervention, an instance like the mythical strongman, Samson; for his God to intercede one last time on his behalf. Surely this sort of thing had happened outside the realm of the fairy-tales in the bible.

However, there was nothing. Just the humble beginnings of the scourge. A shaming ceremony, inspired by heavy-metal iconography, marijuana, and beer.

He thought he'd befriended at least a couple of the little bastards, as he had on the streets, by overlooking some of their more venal indiscretions, warning them of the dangers of group masturbation, that it could lead to full-blown faggotdom. But he could see now that their compliance with the changes he'd made at the church wasn't a positive response to structure and discipline, but a ruse to lull him into a state of complacency with his false accomplishment that he had not tamed the sons of bitches but was now the helpless keeper, trapped in their cage. One of them tore the clerical collar from his throat, and put it around his, skipping around his compatriots like a pansied version of Martin, while mock admonishing the congregation with a stern wag of his finger. There was something oddly adorable about them, and their pageantry, Martin thought. They were only twelve and thirteen, some only wee, eleven-year-olds, and would still be playing at war, building forts, lighting fires, and cultivating perfectly innocent crushes, if not for their corruption at the hands of Kilty. They were no more dangerous than the lollipop-wielding munchkins in the Wizard of Oz if he squinted just right. However, they were unable to shake off the taint, to remind themselves that this was just a bad trip, where even the most mundane things took on an evil aspect—full of dread and annihilation. To hold on for dear life, until the rapture, and frenzied zealousness of the mental-mob wore off.

They took turns slashing at his flabby stomach with curb-sharpened pocket knives and licking the trickles of blood with the pierced and mutilated tips of their tongues. Much mirthful and childish hair-pulling, many delighted punches, and kicks to the groin later, Kilty put a stop to the junior bacchanalian festivities and summoned them to take up his chair. Then with a wave of his hand, freed Martin from his grasp, and allowed the bedeviled priest's limp body to slide down the wall to the ground. However, before he could raise himself to his feet, and make one last charge through them, and out the door for help, the leering midgets were upon him: hog-tying and hoisting him upon their bony little shoulders.

'Why, my God, why me?' Martin cried out, as always

bemoaning his fate as being a perennial pain in the ass, and forever a fickle friend.

'You're not forsaken, Father Martin. Far from it. Relish your role, as written by the divine author of all things, in its book of shadows. Play it to the hilt. The left paths you've taken were predetermined to lead you to this very place, for me to fulfill my fate—a cog in my destiny. Like Judas before you, you've always taken the money on top of any personal satisfaction you might've gained, in meting out your brand of swift, but corrupt justice.

With that pronouncement, and under cover of night, the satanic minstrel show shambled off to the church basement and the temple behind the false wall. From his vantage point on the makeshift King carrier, Martin thought the boys looked cute, like malevolent versions of the dwarves, dancing around the maypole in the Men Without Hats, Safety Dance music video.

Chapter 9

They were twenty-one thousand feet up a mountain called Kanchenjunga but expedited by Englishman

during balderdash sessions in its abbreviated form: K2.
Aleister was entranced; watching a younger, more virile,
and much more hirsute version of himself, duke it out
with another member of the expedition. It was hard for
Tom to distinguish a winner of the scuffle. The
name-calling, slapping, and hair-pulling looked more
like a tiff amongst little girls than a fight between two
grown men. Nevertheless, something was settled, and
the rest of the party, consisting of what looked to be
several Europeans, and a smattering of the ever-smiling
and compliant Sherpas, hastily disassembled their tents,
gathered up their supplies, and descended the mountain.

Eventually, after a long time spent sulking in his tent
and feverishly jotting something down in his diary,
distant screams could be heard, and the thunder of a tidal
wave of snow cascading down the mountain
reverberated throughout the valley. Aleister the younger,
didn't so much as flinch, and merely extinguished his
lard-fuelled lamp, and retired for a long nap, before
descending himself with a couple of the leftover
Sherpas. Aleister watched in disgust as his callow,
insolent version, stomped in a tantrum down a little path
cut into a sheer cliff face, endangering himself, and the

few foolhardy members of the party left to aid him in his descent.

Aleister's current incarnation, the older—and he hoped wiser version, looked longingly up at the mountains cloud-locked peak, and levitated toward it, rewriting the history books as he effortlessly floated to the top. The record now showed that he was the first man to surmount the vilified and vaunted peak of Kanchenjunga. He raised his arms in victory, feeling the cold air shoot through his entire being then suddenly stopped, cutting short his revelry, and turned to look in Tom's direction.

'I know you're there Tommy, boy,' he said, with a wicked smile playing on his newly flushed face. It was the first time Tom had ever seen color or signs of genuine life in any of their faces. 'Decided to hitch a ride, eh? 'Tom, now discarnate, stuck in an ectoplasmic state resembling a darker patch of the fog, stirred above the snow.

'You always did like encyclopedias, didn't you Tommy. Now the world will see my name in a far more respectable category, rather than a lowly footnote under F. After this, I shall do the same with Everest, and wipe that drip, Eddie Hillary, from the history books. Then it's off to my boyhood home in Leamington Spa, England, for a good beating or two from my dear-old nanny. Egypt; to get back my copy of the Goetia and make several amendments to The Book of the Law, and bugger Rose, for old times sake. I'll skip Corfu. That was an aberration. My thinking had gone septic from ingesting cat feces and being skint. Finally, back to Boleskine House, Scotland, to complete my destiny; the great operation.'

Tom knew then that he was about to suffer the same fate as the scientist and the Dahlia: like the demise of his son's video game characters after he'd upgrade the console and shut the old one off for good. Put away in the dark corner of the crawl space, that kind of oblivion. The facet of this mythical dimension that he dreaded the most would be the absence of those things we seek in our relationships with other people, a bit of stimulating, sometimes even enlightening conversation, and if one was lucky, a sharing of knowledge. The only difference between Aleister and the rest of the world was he hoped to find this succor from the spirits, rather than his fellow man.

Appealing to his vanity, and knowing that Aleister was driven by his need for fame in any form, and notoriety above everything else, he attempted to point out the one flaw in his master plan, that might lead him to allow Tom to continue along as a passenger on Aleister's magical mystery tour of his past.

'Even if you do complete the great operation, who's going to know about it? There won't be any witnesses and therefore no history. No proof of it happening whatsoever.'

Aleister felt a pang of rage similar to the one he felt when Willy Yeats had denied him initiation into the inner circle of the Golden Dawn and made a mental note to pop by the old headquarters to smote him—and his former mentor, Mathers while he was at it, before continuing to the Loch.

'Wisdom is the solitary satisfaction gained from one's accomplishments,' said Aleister. 'Everest and Yeats...and Mathers, mustn't forget Mathers, will be my last bit of naughtiness—a much-needed indulgence before focusing on my one true purpose. Then I won't need recognition from the annals of your kind. Soulless meat-puppets.' He punctuated this statement with phlegm from the depths of his lungs and spat.

'And now for your treat, Tommy boy. A tidbit regarding your stepson, Michael.'

Tom felt a frost from the word. He froze, tinkling in the wind as he became crystalline. It was the designation that his progeny was a mere stepson.

'Pity you allowed him to be buggered by the same priest who violated you as a boy, Thomas. I'd have him for the ritual, but he's far too jaded now for that. Probably bugger the whole thing up.'

This last revelation thrust the once desired memories back into his consciousness. All at once he was enlightened. He, Thomas, now little more than a whiff of spirit-stuff, had been in life nothing more than a byproduct of terrible abuse. His entire being a consequence of repressed trauma, manifesting in his desire never to make a wave, ruffle another's feathers, or stand out in any way—until the mid-life crisis. It meant absolute anonymity in life. For his safety he'd chosen to be a nobody—a nothing, and that's the way he'd wanted it. It had cost him individuality, true love, and his son's welfare. Is that what everyone did in the face of a terrible secret? Had his stepson's light gone out too, and is that what he meant by jaded? That's why he'd ended up in limbo. He'd left the most important thing in life unfulfilled: his true will, which was little more than the happiness gained from self actualization. He was already oblivious.

'I leave you to your version of the temptation. Except, in this case, you can have at it: a forty times infinity fast in this desert of ice, and interminable contemplation. Look at it this way, Tom, even this is better than nothingness, and at least they'll retain their memories of you. Like this little, almost invisible pock on my cheek.'

Aleister pulled a thing the size of a pill from his rear-end and tossed it in the air. The Wormhole opened, and Tom could see a beautiful English Manor house on the other side.

'Pleasure before business, I always say,' he said with a chuckle, stepping through the quivering threshold of the window as it closed behind him, causing only a slight disturbance in the trajectory of the falling snow, and popping into nothingness.

Chapter 10

If Tom's neighbors, in an interview with a news crew after he'd going postal and was subsequently identified as the lone gunman in the commission a mass murder at a fast food restaurant. If asked about the anonymous, lowly data entry clerk that he was; they all would have uttered the same—seemingly scripted response: he seemed like a nice guy, perfectly normal, disconcertingly quiet perhaps but a good neighbor who kept to himself nevertheless.

Never caused any trouble. Never saw it or him coming. It's the same thing said of serial killers, but sadly true in Tom's case, and probably the same thing his friends, family, teachers, and bosses would say in response to the query.

This place reminded him of the enlightenment promised by the Shao Lin master in his stepson's martial arts video game, and hell, in the Gideon bibles he'd glance through and then inexplicably steal, on one of his many meaningless business trips. It wasn't much different from his life on the other side. This thought at first gave him a fragment of comfort from its familiarity but then reminded him of the stark absence of even those insignificant things, inauspicious personages, and rote activities, to act as temporary diversions from the bleakness of his current reality. He prayed for the madness to come now; imploring the Gods to have mercy and allow him to jump forward to a state of blissful ignorance so as not to suffer the preceding stage of tortuous cognizance that he was going insane.

Then came a flutter amongst the static sound of falling snowflakes, and a manilla envelope fell in a gentle back and forth motion to the ground before him. The words appeared before him without him opening it, like neon-red subtitles, superimposed on the gusts of wind and sleet. It was a form suicide note to his wife and stepson. He remembered getting it off an assisted suicide website for a small donation. It was more of an insult to loved ones than a farewell. Full of Hallmark sentiments and broad horoscope-like generalities, totally void of real emotion and remorse. However, at the last second, he knew he'd changed his mind. With the screaming of the train, babies, and the look of astonishment on the face of the rockabilly's face, causing his cigarette to drop from his mouth, came an unexpected and overwhelming peace from resignation and surrender to the reality of his situation. At that moment he no longer feared anonymity, death, or anything for that matter. He knew, looking up from his mashed remains—nothing more than glistening entrails, and unidentifiable organs (he'd flunked biology), that he'd punched the tilt button.

Esmeralda was one of those obliging neighbors that succeeded in getting their face on the news that night. It was one of those quaint—regional tragedies; padding for news nights, scant on war, terrorism, or acts of God. A bone tossed to the disgruntled weatherman. For though he was only a lowly meteorologist (a bottom feeder in the news world), the ratings always peaked during his segments, and thus he'd been granted this assignment due to it being a contract year and their fear of losing his, Ron Howard-like appeal to the competition.

She found Tom's blandness rather appealing—sexy even. The perfect antidote to her quirky awesomeness. She'd watch him when he'd collect the morning paper, walk the dog, or come home at night from work, and contemplate before entering the house, whether he should go inside or go away for good. It was her observation of these little things that made her invaluable to Gaylord, and a favorite gossip at the neighborhood cracker, cheese, box wine, and yoga parties. She thought he'd make for a perfectly submissive coital plaything; an adjunct to her indiscretions with Gaylord.

Lately, she'd been lacing her weed, with cocaine, and the usual results; a tendency toward risky propositions of sex with men who gave off the vibe of being contentedly married, but whom she knew telepathically had given up on the prospect of ever being happy again, and more dangerous forms of nigromancy. She'd had forbidden carnal knowledge of the token one that attended her high school, but none regrettably since.

She'd found a copy of the Hermetic Corpus at the library, mistakenly returned to the shelf for herbal remedies for whatever might be ailing you—right next to a book on homemade salves for herpes. Convenient for her as she'd recently suffered a flare-up in her nether region (or as she jokingly referred to it—her almost never region). Gaylord had forbidden her from dabbling in these, much more dangerous forms of magic; not for her sakes, but for the preservation of the material world, as there was no telling what she, in her compromised mental state, might unleash upon it.

She felt whirly-birds of anticipation in her deflating stomach. She'd recently terminated a pregnancy using one of the herbal remedies prescribed in the book, and it worked, but the gift—not so much. She cracked open the sour-smelling volume to the chapter on Necromancy. Good thing she'd bought several articles of Tom's clothing from his wife's garage sale in anticipation for this day, she thought, this being a required field to fill in before she could proceed to the next. Cat skins were the preferred talisman for the spell, but Esmeralda wouldn't so much as touch a hair on the hairless bodies of her beloved familiars (Who'd vamoosed as a precaution). She got out her wand from the box of doo-dads and lit bushels of dried lavender, sage, and incense. Though it was a warm and sunny day, night poured on to her frayed Persian carpet, and her cats began to yowl their pained forebodings that something was upon them from the safety of the neighbor's house across the street.

Hermes appeared to her as he always did to aspirants foolish enough to summon him, for what in magic circles is considered to be the ultimate abomination. The spell to end all abracadabra-to defy God's, warning that one should never have any Gods before him (thus based on the current level of worldwide narcissism, justifying a sequel to the great flood, the reanimated Charlton Heston starring in The Greatest Flood Ever). She wanted to play Goddess, and like the Christ with Lazarus before her, raise Tom from the dead. Willing to sacrifice her very soul because she was horny, and in the mood for some of that good-old necro-loving. '

From the haze of smoke, she saw the figure of an ancient man appear, wearing the hooded robe of a Benedictine monk, staring at her with unmoved crimson eyes that burned into hers. He was holding forth a tome, bigger than any bible she'd ever seen and pointed a long, bony finger in her face. He began to speak with gravelly solemnity (until he had to clear his throat and raise his voice to over the Enya album she insisted on blasting during evocations), a warning to all who dare summon him for such nefarious purposes. 'When thou art come into the land which the Lord thy God giveth thee, thou shalt not learn to do according to the abominations of those nations. There shall not be found among you anyone who maketh his son or his daughter to pass through the fire, or who useth divination, or an observer of times, or an enchanter, or a witch, or a charmer, or a consulter with familiar spirits, or a wizard, or a necromancer. For all who do these things are an abomination unto the Lord, and because of these abominations, the Lord thy God doth drive them out from before thee. Do you wish to proceed, bone conjurer?'

'Fuck yeah,' she said, as she snorted a long line from her scrying mirror and clapped like a kid with a sugar rush at a two-bit magic show.

Tom was figuring out infinity when suddenly he felt a thrill of wind, like the lightspeed trajectory of a roller coaster in a loop—rush through to his cytoplasmic core, and Whoosh. He was blown from the snowy climes of Kanchenjunga and thrust back into his shattered body. He felt pain for the first time in forever, from every stitch and staple that'd been woven and punched, in a bold but futile attempt on the part of the young gun mortician to form a semblance of a human body. A corpse enough to justify his widow's expenditure on a cheap coffin.

The masterpiece, his piece de resistance that would never be seen by anyone but him. He was a fan of slasher films and hoped one day the special effects artists to whom he sent pictures of his more gruesome transformations, would accept his request for an apprenticeship, rather than threaten to contact the authorities and have his license revoked. He was sure his time had come with the resurgence of the Zombie genre. It was only a matter of time until Tom Savini or Rick Bottine extended an invitation for him to join them in Hollywood, and his creations would grace movie and tv screens around the world, rather than buried, to rot in obscurity.

Tom felt the cold of the fridge and slab, making his bones shudder and crack back into place. He was sputtering to life, like the abandoned jalopy: a forty-one Nash—real gangster, with suicide doors and seats like easy-boys, his father stashed in the garage. The one 'Tommy-boy' would hotwire for night-long joyrides through the hush of the neighborhood, pick up his future wife, and for a split-second, he'd be the boss-kid in town because he had a ride with a radio, and a chick to boot.

He'd cruise by the other kids' houses, hoping one of them would see him and pass it on to another, a whispered revelation of his delinquency and coolness. However, his rebellion would remain a secret—anonymous as ever. He'd have to be satisfied with getting laid in the back seat by his surprisingly ravenous girlfriend, the home economics master, and two-time typing champion.

His skin was a crispy-critter, and his guts were squishy and raw in the middle like a burnt sausage. He felt around the stainless steel sarcophagus for a light or a way out but hit a bell instead. It rang loudly like a fire alarm to alert staff if one of their stiffs was still alive. Luckily, Jake, the budding effects kid, had decided to smoke a doobie out back before hitting the road and came running. If his boss found out that he'd rigged these funeral bells to the refrigerators, he'd be toast for sure. Jakes' heart was beating his chest like the one-fingered punches his older cousin would give him in the basement, as a prelude to pinning him to the ground and dangling loogies over his face. The dope usually had a calming effect on his attention deficit and hyperactivity disorders, allowing him to concentrate for more extended periods than his fellow embalmers, but was now making him super-paranoid that he was having a heart attack.

'Hello,' Jake croaked in the dark, swearing he could hear the-ha-ha-ha-ch-ch-ch, from Friday the 13th. The bell went off again, causing him to squeeze out a little pee and turtle a nubbin' of his double cheeseburger.

'Jesus Christ,' he exhaled loudly. Like when he blew burps in the faces of his co-workers. 'What the fuck?'

Tom's throat felt as if a semi-truck had skidded to a halt and blown its tires against his tonsils, but through the rawness managed a pained-faint, 'Hello.'
Jake's hearing was hyper-attenuated, and he could hear the blood pumping and thumping his noggin'.

Another weak and protracted—'Help.'

All of Jake's thoughts were in slow motion, allowing him to freeze frame specific moments. The first was auditory and echoed: 'There's no fucking way this is happening, man, man, man!' The second, a brief scene from his spec-script for a much-needed re-re-reboot of a George Romero zombie movie: Our hero Jake, getting his brains eaten out by a Milf-teacher. Always a favorite masturbatory fantasy. An oldy but a goody. A classic rerun for inspiration. Before the third option could unfold, he was on the microwave-sized body refrigerator doors, frantically wrenching them open to locate the source of the raspy pleas for help.

Tom had flipped onto his stomach and was staring at him with milky, cataract-eyes, trying to blink Jake into focus. He'd always been color blind but was now seeing the world through one of the camera filter apps on his phone: the one for blasting away wrinkles and magically made every woman's eyebrows look like Groucho Marx's. Jake felt a mixture of terror and exhilaration on seeing Tom; his masterwork, come to life. He wanted to scream 'Fuck man, it's alive!' but squealed and weed a little more instead. It may not have been his work that had reanimated Tom, but Jake had succeeded in making him look damned good—for pig slop. He jumped back as Tom pulled himself along the slab into the light, and grabbed a scalpel for protection. He kept the fire ax in full view, knowing that if this zombie made a move for him, he was going to have to do some major-ass chopping. Bummer I'm on comedown mode, he thought, then fumbled around for his cell phone thinking: this would make a fucking excellent audition tape for Savini, and get like a trillion hits on Youtube.

Tom knew what the kid was up to, and had no problem with it, but needed him to calm down before he dropped dead from a stroke.

'You can take as many pictures as you want, but first, you gotta do me a couple of favors, kay?' He wanted to keep everything he said short, sweet, and stupid, as Tom didn't know how long his voice was going to last, and because the kid looked like he'd fried the few brain cells God had given him on kitchen sink quality drugs.

'Coupla' solids, kay. I can do that.'

The poor, stupid kid, Tom thought. Why doesn't he just run? Anyone stuck into this fucked up, bizarre, beyond surreal scenario should run screaming for the safety of the booby-hatch. Then he remembered; it was a generational thing, and the lengths kids these days would go to, the hard graft for their fifteen minutes of fame, risking life and limb to capture that tiny moment in time that amused, amazed, or grossed out their target audience.

'Can you walk, man?' Jake asked, wiping the bloodshot and wonderment from his eyes.

'I don't know,' Tom groaned. 'Gimme a hand.'

He had to stifle vomit at the thought of his duty to

Esmeralda, an instinctual drive now, as automatic as morning wood. (On inspection the kid had been pretty kind in that department).'I borrowed some from a dude that had more than enough,' said Jake.

The very idea of having to comply with that dirty hippies sexual peccadilloes made the embalming fluid in his insides spin like the first time he'd gotten drunk on an unholy shit-mix of anything he could find underneath the kitchen sink. Then he offered the kid the one sure thing, the souped-up engine that drove every young, desperate, zit-faced male on the planet: to get laid, in exchange for his services for the night.

Jake got him to his feet and made Tom fist pump to seal the deal.

'Got a car?' Tom asked, dreading the thought of having to keep this wastrel focussed and entertained for the evening.

'You bet. The van in the back. Where we, goin'?'

'Seventh and Greenwich Avenue. Mulry Square.'

Then, back in line with his pre-death hijacking of third-rate, hard-boiled aphorisms: 'and make it snappy, kid.'

They went to Mulry Square, but the Diner wasn't

there. Just an empty lot next to a gas station. So it was true: *Nighthawks*—the painting, was just an amalgamation of real and imagined places. Figments of Hopper's romantic, painterly mind. He'd struck an archetype. A gold-rich vein, spidering its way from the collective unconscious, resulting in a rush on exploitation. Countless counterfeit-quality copies had infiltrated American consciousness, resulting in the now rapidly fading glory of Hopper's version and Tom's, in a parallel universe.

Tom knew what he had to do, sure as breathing. He had to destroy Hopper's original to preserve the Diner. Anything was better than the black and white proposition of heaven or hell, maybe even Oblivion.

They hopped into Jake's shag-carpeted love machine and blasted Iron Maiden's, *Number of the Beast* as they tried to peel out of the parking lot but only succeeded in executing a lame fishtail before speeding off into the night.

Aleister rode the astral highway like a speed-drunk Yank, driving the Autobahn for the very first time. He landed in a back alley in London, where he remembered the headquarters for the Hermetic Order of the Golden

Dawn to be. He imagined himself a magical revolutionary, triumphantly returning home from a long exile to the far reaches of the universe, after a failed coup d'etat, but was still perceived by contemporaries as having been nothing more than a spoiled, self-indulgent, petulant rich kid. Not beyond abusing black magic means to get his way, and incurring the ire of Mathers (his former mentor and co-conspirator in a bid to take over the Golden Dawn), and the poet, W.B Yeats, along the way. These disagreements became downright nasty at times, with each Magus utilizing his brand of magic to exact revenge against the other. This particular battle had been left unfinished, at least in Aleister's mind, and started as a result of a loan he'd made to Mathers, with an eye toward him securing lodgings to start a new magical order. The plan had never come to fruition, and Mathers ended up frittering the funds away on indulgences for his wife.

Aleister dusted himself off and hid in the shadows from passersby as he inserted the wormhole into his anus. He peered around the corner, waiting for his younger self to stop his blustering and posturing and piss off.

'Out of the way, old man,' the lankier version of Aleister said, as he brushed past his older self, and disappeared into the hustle of a frigid London night.

Aleister threw open the temple doors and presented himself in sweepingly grand fashion to a perplexed Mathers, who was buried in a game of chess with an invisible demon.

'Crowley?' he said, looking up from intense contemplation of his next move. Then shot up from his seat and shook his head in bafflement.

'Yes, it is I. Finally returned, a century later, from many realms away, Conquering Purgatory, Kuchanjenga, Everest, and home again.

After their last ill-fated meeting, Mathers had sent a psychic vampire, a succubus in the form of a beautiful woman, to tempt Aleister, and suck the life force from him, but Aleister had used her evil against her, and smote the crone back to oblivion whence she came, with her own power.

'Ah, you've taken up time travel. But not mastered it, I see, based on the wreckage standing before me.'

'I've conquered Physics, you Munz-watcher. It is not a pseudo-science fiction: not the sleight of hand of our lowly secret Chiefs, but the conveyance for the Gods themselves. You were nothing but a charlatan who took advantage of the innocence, and naive enthusiasms of my younger self, and now you shall pay. I will banish you to oblivion.'

Mathers harrumphed and took up a magical fighting stance. Something like a Kung Fu kata, but much more effete.

'Science? Novice, have you forgotten the taste of Coronzon? Shall I summon her here again? Fear can never be destroyed. So tremble, quake, and above all, offer me your thanks. The world will change when you lay eyes on this fear.'

Aleister laughed, pulled out the wormhole, and ripped it open, 'Voila.' There was only a cold, whispering black void on the other side. He grabbed a simpering Mathers by the ear and threw him in.

'You are gone, and mine will be true—are forgotten.' He could hear Mathers echoing screams as he disappeared into a spiraling vortex of nothingness, leaving only cold-darkness in the window.

He shut it, inserted back into its usual hiding place, then took a moment to look around his old haunt. It had once been a golden palace of aspiration and ultimate wisdom. Now he saw it with the cynicism of older eyes. It was nothing more than the dusty digs of some failed political party. A cast-off lease their motley crew had picked up for a song, and turned into a temple for their dreams. It stunk of rot and mold now, and he wondered how they had ever seen it as anything else but a shambles. He turned to go but stopped at the sunspot that had once been the place for Mathers portrait, smiling as it disappeared, and his picture slowly materialized, taking its rightful place on the wall.

A pipe had burst, flooding the floor with gray matter. The Invisibles dutifully mopped it up, and quickly, but the atrophy continued to spread. The razed tiles now skittered about like pucks on an air hockey table. The Wurlitzer was on the fritz and had to be struck, Fonzie-style to get the old girl going, and the coffee was fully formed jello. The Raven was perched atop the old radio tower and the hellhounds circled and howl-whimpered, in anticipation of the diners imminent collapse and for the free for all to begin. Hubbard and the gang were trapped inside and itching to get out, hitting each other up for loans of shekels against favors—nothing was off limits.

Captain Ron saw opportunity in the existential anxiety induced by their peril, and rustled up some coffee cans from the back, jerry-rigging a working model of his most infamous contribution to quackery, the new-fangled probe of the subconscious, the E-meter. He demonstrated its power to identify what he called Engrams. Supposedly, these were the mental image pictures that prevented one from attaining the state of 'Clear' and thus the full potential of their souls as fully operational 'Thetans.' He paid particular attention to the bored and bemused celebrities that had assembled around his table, who boisterously enthused that they'd finally found 'it,' and wondered where the devil they could get their hands on one of the billion-year contracts he was offering. To sign away their rights to live out paying occupations in subsequent incarnations—reminded them of the old studio system.

As members of the Sea-Org, they would even get snazzy outfits that resembled the naval uniforms for some banana republic, and compensated with further courses on Hubbard's 'technology,' and the satisfaction of saving the world one lost soul at a time. Tab thought he'd look sharp as he cruised the seven seas, no longer having to wait for some costumed affair, or play pretend when he'd go on furlough to one of the 'funny' sailor bars.

'See, Tab, your problems stem from repressed homosexuality. However, you're in luck, for a few shekels I can cure you. Just like that Travolta fellow, and Tom Cruise. Couldn't cure his other little problem, but you know what they say—it's what you do with it that counts.'

The building groaned as if it was alive, weary and giving in to the burden of absorbing so much ego-mania. Some looked outward at the snapping jaws of the wolves, and the infinite eyes of the bird of prey, black as the hearts of hell, reflecting all and betraying nothing of its thoughts—the others downward, at the inevitable.

Satan was depressed. He cursed himself for his terminal inability to enthuse about anything. The playing of Mandingo, to the hordes of sweaty and surprisingly compliant southern-belles that crossed county lines to sample his kielbasa sized member, and sexual acrobatics, had lost its wicked-appeal. Though he'd succeeded in burying many loads of his molten essence in their cavernous wombs, and thus ensuring the world of a never-ending supply of one-hit wonders, child stars, inventors of faddist exercise equipment—and they're irritating, infomercial shills, he was utterly and unequivocally bored. The only thing he'd never done was blow up the whole kit and kaboodle to smithereens but had been beset by the unrelenting temptation to do so. Like a kid who 'accidentally' tickles their sibling, hard enough to turn their fingers into instruments of torture, or a sudden, uncalled-for, slap to their face, that smarted enough to make them cry, to stick a finger in a socket or a knife in the toaster. The temptation gnawed at him until he just wanted to do it; get it over with: to experience the sweet relief from knowing how it felt. However, he couldn't—couldn't just. That would be like 'accidentally' curb stomping your cell phone with the misguided belief that the phone company was obliged to replace it for the bigger, thus better version, he thought. Then he heard the conciliatory maxim of disappointed girlfriends everywhere: It's not the size that matters…'

Aleister blew into London's great pretender to a Parisian-style—bourgeois cafe, where Willy Yeats was bound to be holding court. He'd been rich enough to know and love the real thing, and so only went there back in the day out of a sense of duty to promote himself and his work. Aleister had given a reading of an excerpt from his book of poetry, *White Stains* there, to a shocked audience comprised of wannabee-bohemians, on furlough from Oxford. He never forgave W.B, for the beamingly smug smile he gave in reaction to the outrage and walk-outs from that evening's presentation. Aleister cringed from a corner table, watching the younger, read from the poetic work that was meant to be a best-seller, a classic to spearhead an early sexual revolution, but had only resulted in Aleister having in having to give copies away to purveyors of 'penny dreadfuls', smut, and his besotted concubines.

He watched his reaction to the audience's revulsion, and profane catcalls. Nasty Victorian-era vitriol, like: be gone with your vile pornography—you syphilitic cad, and calling him a two-bit whooperup, and no-good purveyor of mutton. Stuff like that. Then in a hissy-fit, stomp off to the opium den to lick his wounds, pussy, and smoke a bowl of the Dragon's breath. He loathed Willy B. but didn't let the little-fucker take his power away from him because he knew the real reason why he hated England's, self-proclaimed, poet laureate, though he would rather eat shit and die than admit this fact to another.

Yeats, unlike he, had gained fame and genuine respectability from his poetry, the very thing that he'd so craved, yet had eluded him his whole creative life. He considered his work superior to anything Yeats had written, and free from the stagnant and maudlin romanticism typical of the bog-trotters contributions to the poetic canon. Yeats, was also instrumental in the rejection of Aleister's petition to gain admittance to the second order of the Golden Dawn, where all the juicy secrets were reputedly kept. Aleister also considered himself the true heir to the Byronic mantle and legacy, having truly lived, loved, and bled for his muse, rather than expostulating from the safety of imagined, tragic scenarios, made-up infatuations, and odes to the unrequited puppy-love, of Willy's, lowly limericks. He'd learned his lesson on the dire consequences of self-delusion, repressed hatred, and misuse of indirect action, from the tragic death of Raoul Loveday, his accomplice in all things 'unutterably vile' back in Cefalu Italy, and so owned it.

He ordered two absinthes and pulled the chair out from one of Yeats slathering sycophants.

'My dear Willy, how goest, it?'

'You left and are returned, a bloated old man,' Yeats said, with venomous relish. He looked to his companions for approval, and they acquiesced, covering their mouths with silk kerchiefs as they tittered. He was ever so slight and bespectacled; a little worm of a man that the much broader Aleister, wanted to squash like a bug.

'Astral travel has not been kind to you, Crowley. Did you not know you're meant to retain your current age and rank on returning from such journeys, not slink into a state of utter decrepitude and impoverishment.' Aleister placed a hand on the shoulder of one of the Bon vivants, seated at the table, and began to squeeze hard.

'Congrats on Kuchanchenga, though I'm sure your mountaineering exploits hardly do anything to assuage your failings as a poet and a magician.'

The toadie in Aleister's vice-like grip grew wane from the pressure, as Aleister's aura turned into a blue flame, and tried to excuse himself but was rammed back into his seat with a blink of Aleister's eyes.

'We musn't forget Everest.'

He raised his glass and shot back the drink, while Yeats, noisily sipped.

Yeats continued. 'That's right; you never did get past the preliminary stages of your study. Are you aware of the reasons why?'

He stood up to his full five feet and counted on the power of his poetry to convey his inner stature.

'Your black magic is no match for mine. My white light is a beacon that illuminates your true nature, and burns away the vile abomination of your lesser, niggardly conjurings.'

Aleister immediately thought of Pat Boone's wonderbread version of 'Tutti Frutti,' and laughed.

'And no amount of alcohol will change my mind,' he said, finishing his drink, and bidding him adieu with a wave of his hand.

'That's not my intention. I want you to be sober as a judge when you meet your fate.'

With that, Aleister released his grip from the flunkey's shoulder and strode outside. On surveying the establishment—and not being able to discern whether the smell was the stench of beatniks or the open sewer in front of the building, decided the best course of action would be to swallow the whole sideshow up and shit it into oblivion. He opened the wormhole wide, coaxing it over the building, and guided the void over it.

He could hear the bonhomie inside turn shrill, and a negro singing a southern spiritual (all the rage in gay Paris) fade out slowly as they imploded into the black hole, and with one last flash of Yeat's white light, disappeared into the void.

Aleister rode the rooftop to the edge of oblivion then leaped off over Egypt.

Immediately he infused his dwindled inheritance with Yeat's, Nobel prize earnings, depositing them in a Swiss bank, and had the account number seared into his consciousness. They would emerge in a later incarnation—on his skin, in the form of a birthmark, and be mistaken for the sign of the beast of revelation. He just thought the numbers easy to remember in a jiff.

In the Giza Necropolis; a luxury hotel conveniently located across the street from the pyramids; in a lavish suite, adorned with all the finery and accouterments befitting a visiting Sheik (the style he traveled in when he was still flush with his inheritance). He watched with fascination the young Mr. Crowley, smooth and taut (he couldn't remember the last time the crotch of his pants weren't a sling for his prolapsed testicles) transcribe, *The Book of the Law,* as dictated to him by the God, Horus; and the basis for hid homebrew religion: *Thelema.* His then-wife, Rose, was there, positively beatific in her capacity of the scarlet woman; naked, giddy, and flush from spirits, as she knelt before him. Aleister, truly missed her, more than any other of the copious, women he had used throughout his life, and was jealous of the younger for a moment, before coming to his proverbial senses, and waiting to see what had become to his priceless book of magic.

He watched the scene unfold—and it did; proceeding exactly as he suspected it had all those years ago.

That it had been while subsumed in the trance that Cecil Gaylord, his once trusted secretary, snuck into the antechamber and stole the Goetia, fleeing from the scene, the authorities, and Egypt, soon after—and not seen again—till now.

He'd stolen Aleister's most cherished possession; the

culmination of many lifetimes of work, a book of shadows that he'd written in his blood and bound in the skins of stillborn babies. That was the bookbinders boast. He specialized in forbidden texts (mostly magic, but a bit of Victorian whalebone corset porn on the side) and claimed to have a wife who he kept in a cage, whose miscarriages were helped along for the express purpose of providing him with the leather for the books, but was probably really tomcat or stray dog.

Then presently, as the young Aleister continued to scribble manically away, and Gaylord was about to abscond with the book, Aleister the old, wise to Gaylord's treachery, emerged from his hiding spot, a hanging Persian tapestry. Interceding on the younger's behalf, he grabbed Gaylord from behind, and slit his throat with a ceremonial dagger he'd found lying around. He dispatched him swiftly and silently, like a silk road assassin, so as not to disturb the young prophet from his most important work. Oblivion is too good for you motherfucker, Aleister thought, as Gaylord gasped and fell to his knees, clutching at his throat. He pinched the yawning wound to quell the torrential blood-flow, but it refused to adhere and flapped madly between his drenched fingers, like a torn sail in the frothy wind of every desperate breath, and so he slumped—straight to hell.

It was strange having a threesome with himself, but he was able to get through it by focusing on giving one last farewell buggering to Rose, and after he'd finished, while the others slept, pushed off to make a few corrections to the manuscript, leaving the rest of it to his younger self.

He knew of an undiscovered tomb containing treasures to rival Tutankhamen's, but decided, somewhat oddly, to forego his usual piggishness in such matters, and be satisfied with K2, Everest, and his Nobel prize for literature...for now. He gave himself one last gentle kiss on the cheek and was off to the final destination on his whistle-stop tour of the astral plane: Boleskine and the fulfillment of his true will. Was it kismet that Cher's, If I could turn back time, was the soundtrack to his latest triumph? Courtesy of a camel herder's transistor radio, duct taped to his poor beast's neck. No matter, he thought, as the wind whiffled his jowls and couldn't help but hum along.

Chapter 11

'This is a fuck'in trip man. I—am giving a ride—to a
reanimated cadaver—to the museum of all places. I'm
assuming to appreciate art and shit. Jesus fucking Christ.
Toke?'

'Sure is Kid,' Tom said, but just said no to the dope.
He liked calling someone else 'kid' for once. Whether it
was age appropriate or not, everyone else did him. He
recalled an incident with the rocker in the subway—the
punk calling him kid then to fuck off. After he'd asked
him how the rocker did it—how he'd summoned the
courage to assert his individuality so cooly. And how he
smiled sheepishly and did fuck off, but wanted to kill the
rocker—throw him in front of the train for being such a
dickhead but of course didn't, and had a feeling this was
the story of his past life.

He never went in for the marijuana, it made him
paranoid, and he'd usually end up either under or
jogging around the dining room table, thinking that a
sudden burst of activity would shock his heart into a
regular, less ponderous rhythm, thus averting a slow
motion heart attack.

Esmeralda had tried to tempt him into her shanty once, with a cannon-sized spliff, and a cup of oolong tea, but politely declined her offer, finding the stench of cat piss, patchouli oil, and the Eagles, a little bit much. 'What's your story?' asked Tom. He knew Jake was far too young to have cobbled together anything resembling a meaningful life story but gave it a shot. It would probably be the last one he'd ever hear thanks to that witchy-woman; her crush—turned obsession with him and her misuse of the necromancy spell. Aleister had warned him about the efficacy and danger of that kind of blacker than black magic. That while it could set you free from whatever realm you were trapped, it came at a terrible price—one's very soul. During a follow up conversation over yet another cup of coffee and a pile of pie, he explained the soul as being a combination of three things: sentience, individuality, and our true will.

Jake, sputtered out half a super-toke and turned down the music.

'Well, let's see, uh..., uh—well, I'm a mortician, as you know. You came in looking like humpty dumpty if he was a bucket of entrails tossed from the Willis Tower, and I put you back together again. Did a righteous job, if

I do say so myself.'

Jake was in a stoned, lovesick reverie; swooning over the prettiness of his miraculous concealment of Tom's traumatic injuries. Hell, he thought, the guy comes into the mortuary in separate containers—Chinese takeaway style, and—swerved to avoid crashing head-first into an oncoming semi-truck.

'You mind if I grab a few selfies and some video with you later?'

'Nope, Tom said,' turning the music right off, and keeping an eye on the road, shattered hand at the ready to steer the van himself if need be. There'd be no second chance at this, and his wife would probably choose the cheaper option of cremation, the second time around.

'I'm trying to get in with a special effects crew. Y'know Rob Botine, Rick   Baker, or Tom Savini.'

'Cool,' Tom said.

Tom thought he looked more like one of Jack Pierce's famous monsters of Hollywoodland, like Frankenstein's monster than one of the antiheroes from slasher porn. 'Let's see, what else, oh yeah, and I'm in therapy for Pyromania. My folks think I'm going to turn into a bonafide serial killer. My therapist says it's one of the points on the Macdonald triad.'

That explained the odor of gasoline coming from the back.

'The other two are animal torture and bed-wetting.' Tom hoped Jake was only an incontinent firestarter and checked to see if he was wearing special pants.

'Somebody kidnapped my dog Blue, and my folks thought it was me, so they won't let me have any more pets—not even a Chia. Rubber sheets—the works, dude.'

'So you like starting fires, eh?' Tom said, thinking that the fates had dumped the perfect accomplice right into his lap.

Jake perked up. 'Yeah, sure. I mean, I can tell you cus' yer dead and shit, but its a real turn on, you know. Gets me going.'

Every kid has a fascination with fire, Tom thought, but he didn't whack-off to the little conflagrations he'd lit in the forest back in the day...

'So what about you, man, why'd you do it?'

Good, jumping to the chase, Tom thought.

'Do what?'

'Off yourself, man. I mean, I thought about it tons of times. Would they let me have Slayer playing as they wheeled my body back to the hearse. Who would come to my funeral—would they cry, you know, that kind of shit. But I would've been a bit kinder to myself if you know what I mean. I hear hangings not too bad, and carbon monoxide poisoning puts you to sleep. Why not an overdose on some really good shit, like oxycodone or fentanyl?'

Tom thought about it for a second before answering. He was glad he didn't have to get into the whole epic misadventure and push the kid over the edge, blowing his already fragile and what appeared to be—deep-fried mind.

'I didn't. Pushed,' Tom said, casually—but as a matter of fact.

'By who?'

He picked up the cover for an Iron Maiden cd and pointed to their infamous mascot, *Eddie*, who graced countless t-shirts and posters. There probably wasn't a kid in the world who didn't own something with his image on it at some point during their youth.

'It looked something like that.'

Jake's eyes dilated and widened for the first time during their little joy-ride.

'Holy shit, dude, you serious?'

'Yup.'

'Your wife was looking to bury you in a Catholic cemetery, you know, consecrated ground and everything, but she was told she couldn't, by this Father Kilty guy...it being a suicide and all. He's a real Mr-stickler for the rules.'

Tom wanted to kill Kilty when he was finally allowed to get off the Nighthawk Express. Do it during Mass, in front of a full-house of parishioners, ending the cycle of depravity for now at least, and hoping that it wasn't too late for his son.

The sickness manifested itself in different ways. Some, like Tom, stayed its pure victim, and wouldn't hurt a fly—let alone an innocent child. In life, he made himself small as a toddler, retreating to the safety and predictability of daydreams. So much so, that it became his reality. A sanctuary from the treachery and betrayal of the so-called real world, peopled with characters that espoused ideals that they had no intention of living. He'd rejected any good luck and fortune that came his way as a portent of impending doom. Now in his fantasies, he was the top man at his company; had the 6.5, company car, and the beautiful wife who loved every part of him—even the dirty bits, but instead, was stunted, sullied and shrunken into a tiny lump of brimstone by Kilty's perversions. He'd come to understand himself intuitively because his condition couldn't be explained in words. That was why this thing lay dormant and was kept secret from the world, and why he married his wife: she didn't ask questions. The other kind became like their abusers.

Tom had to prioritize; thus a reunion with his wife didn't make the cut. So off they went to torch one of America's greatest modern masterpieces. Of course, Aleister had suggested that if Tom ever got the chance, to do a few others while he was at it. Mostly British artists, who'd disparaged Aleister's work during his lifetime, and some French paintings, thrown in for good measure. His spite masquerading as principle.

He knew his time was finite, and that as soon as Jake had consummated the spell, by servicing Esmeralda, his body would return to dust and his soul—fade to black. He never felt so all alone and wanted whoever to play Ricky Nelson as they swept up his remains and put them in the dust bin.

'Sweet ride,' Jake said, nodding at a souped-up, jet-black, Chevy Impala that flashed like a blood-soaked steel blade in the flickering, mercury-vapor streetlights. It thundered up beside them, then suddenly swerved toward the passenger side of the van, nudging them into oncoming traffic. Jake saw the driver as the grim reaper, with a cackling, skeletal face, and burning red eyes. Tom saw it for what it was: an earthbound shadow-demon summoned to compel him to fulfill his end of Esmeralda's nefarious bargain.

'I read about this kind of thing, dude.' Jake said as he punched the accelerate and rolled down the window to feel the wind blow through the feathered sides of his mullet.

'Stay calm; fear is what these fucker's feed off. Jake reached toward the glowing console and flipped a switch duct taped to the underside.

'Nitro, baby.'

Tom nodded, 'That's irony—for sure. I'm positive. Yup.'

The ghost car rammed them even harder, leaving Jake no choice but to careen into the opposing lane and weave and wind through the cacophony of horns and headlights and drive-by invective.

Jake yelled, mouthed, and gesticulated instructions even though Tom could hear him just fine. 'Go into the glove box and hand me the cd under the registration.'

He pulled it out, expecting even heavier, death metal, as the new soundtrack for their dilemma, but was shocked to find in his fingers a copy of an album that he hadn't seen since the bad old days of K-tel records. His mother's original had been vinyl and the lullaby for millions of easy-chair bound, old-age pensioners, and the precursor to relaxation, and bliss states by fledgling meditators—the world over: Zamfir.

'Come on, Zamfir. Why not Anne Murray or better yet—Nana Mouskouri?' Tom yelled back, as Jake was seriously deaf.

'Trust me it works. I use it as a soothing balm for skittish chicks that won't put out and pesky, demonic entity types. They can't stand it. Puts them right to sleep. Crank Dat Shit, motherfucker!' And a couple of skips in the disk later, the soothing tones of the pan-pipes blared from the stereo system. An expensive Blaupunkt, as this was the essential component of any teenager's car, coming before gas and even rarer—oil changes in automotive priorities.

To Tom's astonishment, it was working. Not only were they attracting the scorn and derision of every youngblood and their chicks, out for that evening's club crawl, but the chase car had backed off enough for them to return to the proper lane. Tom crawled over the crunchy shag carpeting and watched from the back window as the driver of the phantom Impala shook its head violently back and forth; trying to loosen the easy-listening anthem from its skull. Then the whole hot rod began to vibrate and break into micro-dots of black and white static, before combusting entirely into a windblown cloud of exhaust smoke. Tom crawled back to his seat and they hooped and high-fived.

'See, I told you. Stop fighting the demons, and they become smoking-hot she-angels, bro.'

They were almost there, so Tom turned down the music and began to reluctantly unfurl his plan.

'You okay with one last kick at the gas can? Probably be your biggest one yet. A pyrotechnical extravaganza. I mean…I respect you're in therapy and everything, and I wouldn't want to contravene anything you've accomplished, but I need a solid…bro? This conversation appeared to be going over like death by paper cuts, Jake's expression, while not contemplative, was at least not slack-jawed and drooly, for the first time since they'd unwittingly become the supernatural version of Butch Cassidy and the Sundance Kid.

Tom looked to the jerrycan in the back, sloshing gas around on the carpet with every screeching turn, but didn't dare question the efficacy of Jake's course of treatment because he was asking him to be an accessory to another wanton act of arson and thus, in effect, relapse.

Then Jake's eyes narrowed in conjunction with a smile. He took his hands off the wheel to rub them together as if to warm them over an imaginary fire.

'What are we lookin' at? Y'know, the specs?'

'Specifically, The Art Institute of Chicago,' said Tom.

He thought the sheer size and scope of the target would either be the clincher or the deal-breaker. There were going to be some equally priceless works of art that would be the tragic collateral damage on Tom's farewell tour. *American Gothic*, (he wondered if the wizened old couple were as miserable as the farm they stood guard over), *Water Lilies* by Claude Monet and Van Gogh's:

The Bedroom, plus some Picasso's. The list went on and on. It made him feel like he was committing a heinous sin against humanity, comparable to Hitler's attempted annihilation of 'deviant art' but reassured himself with the conviction that his motives were pure. Sad though, that this altruistic act would only be appreciated posthumously, amongst the silent spirits of the spheres. Jake, on the other hand, didn't give a shit about the where or the why he was too busy, excitedly planning the how.

'The key to this whole thing is gonna be an easy chick—preferably a little chunky and thus slutty.'

'Why fat?' Tom asked, but remembered his moves back in high-school.

'Easier to get on the fly, and they tend to be givers rather than takers. Plus security guards aren't picky that way.'

She sounded like the type of girl Tom, and his buddy landed in high-school: the friendly, amenable, and desperate for any morsel of affection they could get kind. Usually, by the time they'd graduated, they were so used up they had to put a geographic distance between themselves and their hard-earned reputations, either by obtaining an out of state job or by disappearing in the student body of a big college. His wife had been one of them—the pick of the litter. Though with Tom, she'd successfully retrofitted herself into a respectable graduate of a secretarial course, and now heroic, widowed, single mother.

'Why the museum?' Jake said, wondering if Tom's was a divinely inspired act of loonie-ness, or he was just another jolly-seeker like himself. Tom had to think fast, and conveniently remembered the lead singer of his stepson's least favorite heavy metal band—Judas Priest, and the furor amongst the fans when their rock God came out of the closet.

'Well, you know Rob Halford—y'know the lead singer of Judas Priest is gay, right? Jake gave him the stink-eye of death and responded with the conviction and venom a young man who'd tested the veracity of this fact for himself. 'That is a conspiracy theory—*DUDE*! Propagated by right-wing, conservative, Nazi-scumbag, bitches...and lesbians, but do go on.'

'This artist has an exhibition there based on the premise that all the lead singers of heavy metal bands are secret gays, and...

Tom's proposal, with the addition of righteousness to what would seem an act of terrorism to an infidel, gave Jake a semi. 'Yeah, but why do you care,' Jake asked, an air of suspicion in his tone. 'You look like a dead Neil Sedaka fan.'

'Been there, bro, bought the t-shirt back when you were spunk...in your mother's—your dad's...way back, bro. Jake seemed to be satisfied by Tom's on-the-fly explanation, a seed of truth—the key to a fortuitous lie, and they continued plotting.

'Where do we get the fat chick?'

'Gonna have to get a six-pack.'

Tom pulled out the empty pockets of his stocky father-in-law's funeral duds.

'No worries I got a fund for just such occasions. No ID and but you look old enough to be on display as a mummy in the Egypt exhibit. Hey, don't you wanna see your wife or anything?'

Tom checked himself in the rear-view mirror. His cheek seam was coming undone.

'Naw,' Tom said dismissively, 'I was just another piece of display furniture.'

'Got Ya.' Jake sealed the deal with knuckles

He slipped in Def Leppard's, Pyromania, and they both bobbed their heads, Tom, ever so slightly, as they drove through the entrance of a gated community, prowling the neighborhood in search of their bait's address. Tom took it easy on the enthusiasm so his head wouldn't fall off. He was astounded at how all this was unfolding—felt positively empowered. His wife used to sneak out nightly from nearly identical surroundings. He might as well have been picking her up for one of their secret rendezvous. She was a rich kid too. Her nouveau-affluent parents, safe in the assumption that their daughter was conspiring with them to keep up appearances, and never run afoul of the social mores imposed on them by their sudden rise to the upper crust of society.

Because she was a little chunky, got good grades, never broke curfew (to their knowledge), was an innocent who collected Hello Kitty paraphernalia as reward for her academic excellence, but used the expensive Japanese toys as tools of concealment for her contraband, and nearly broke the bank in the process, her daddy always joked.

She also had an obsession for Rob Lowe, and

dutifully collected the suggestive ephemera that came with her fandom. When the news ran the recycled, VHS-quality footage of his dalliance with a minor, she wished it had been her receiving his listless missionary thrusts. Her father hated how she swooned over those pin-ups. It reminded him of his wife's disintegrating collection of Ricky Nelson and Tab Hunter, publicity stills, squirreled away in their hope chest. His wife didn't mind—just didn't like her ruining the wallpaper. It was the same wool, pulled over countless parents eyes for centuries.

Tabitha was fat and she flaunted it. She smelled of a freshly killed cigarette and candy scented perfume. Her chub ran over the waist of her mini-dress slowly, like the head of foam on an over-poured glass of beer. She was the vision of his teenage wife.

'Hey,' she said in general, lighting another cigarette and helping herself to a sweaty can of malt liquor (their only concession to Rap, as it was the anti-matter of heavy metal, but dug the brother's taste in beverages) She cheered with Jake and flashed a look at Tom. 'Fella, you look like you been hit by a truck.'

'Train,' he corrected.

They hung Martin sideways. The boys own twist on perverting the crucifixion, denying him the convention of Christ's execution, and Saint Paul's claim to humility, to suffer the same fate as his master—upside down. Martin suggested a back to front variation, but they dismissed this idea as being impractical for their purpose, and Kilty wanted the whole thing to go off without incident: like a Siegfried and Roy, extravaganza.

They did it by the book. Kilty's black bible, replete with his own scribbled apostilles, taped over the traditional parallelisms.

Funny' thing happened to one of the boys when they went on a run to gather materials for the crucifixion. This time when they broke into the railyard, instead of taking only what they needed—the usual track ties and spikes, they had the good fortune of finding an open, unattended caboose. Most times the back railings were used as guard posts for security personnel, armed with airguns and salted pellets. They hurt like hell, and no magic (as they found out the hard way), made you dodge these projectiles.

They peeked inside to make sure it was abandoned

and clambered aboard, skipping over the usual stashes of beer, drugs, and other essentials for the transient life of a railman, and went straight for the cache of the good stuff, kept hidden in the floorboards: train bombs.

Train bombs were warning signals for the conductors. They were the gold standard of explosives; better than a brick of black cats, cherry bombs, or m-80's. They were the equivalent of a quarter stick of dynamite and detonated by dropping a boulder on them from high up in a treetop. You could sometimes procure them during the Halloween season, but the seller was usually the crazy, fringe dweller, of their clique, and the back-alley sale usually a ruse to rip-off dumb kids of that year's firecracker fund.

Ritchie was one of the stockier boys. The others were wee little—lethal rascals, who made up for their lack of brawn with cunning, mercilessness, and skills at improvising weapons, and then wielding them with the brutality of the Viking hordes. Other gangs, whose patches bordered the boy's turf, left them to get on with the 'devil shit' they got up to at the ungodly hours they chose to roam the streets. If left alone they were no different from a hornets' nest, and generally went about their business without minding others. However, if fucked with, they attacked in a frenzied storm that always ended up with a fatality. What was the purpose of hornets? What was their function on earth? Even killer-bees manufactured honey, didn't they, the other gangbangers mused?

That was the question that made the other gangs steer clear of them. Besides, the other local posse only used graveyards, and their mausoleums, to drink, smoke dope, and get laid. They didn't need those locations for anything business related, and usually left bodies where they fell, as totems of the offense that had been committed against them. It is what it is, they used to say when speed-walking past the church, or while chancing a shortcut through the cemetery.

Ritchie pried open the crate and pulled out one of the red plastic railway detonators. He showed the cigarette pack sized explosive to the others then ran off with it, down the tracks, to an old sledgehammer leaning against a signal light.

He placed the bomb on the rail then grabbed the sledgehammer and held it aloft.

'Hey Ritchie, don't do it, man,' one of them yelled, as

they quick-stepped it toward him. He leered back at them insolently, and smiled vacantly, as he cocked back the hammer a few inches higher. They jogged now in a raggedy drill formation.

'Seriously, man, you're gonna kill yourself if you do that.'

'Fuck off,' and BLAMMO! The sledgehammer kicked back with the speed and force of a trip-hammer, exploding Richie's little head from his broad shoulders in slow-motion. Like a balloon filled with macerated brain, blood, and bone. The sledgehammer gonged and thwacked, as it somersaulted down the tracks, coming to a stop as it became entangled in a barbed wire fence.

A stunned silence fell over their whole world, until his teetering body finally gave up the ghost, and fell with a thud-squish into a pile of its cerebral matter. The hush turned into reams of hysterical laughter, as they investigated the mess that was 'Big Ritch.'

'That was fucking awesome, dude,' one of them crowed, as he dipped a steel-tipped boot into the mush.

'Better than the one in *Scanners*,' another said.
The others nodded silently in agreement.

'Yup.'

Then just left him there. A gift of carrion for the buzzards, and grabbed the stuff for the crucifixion, which would prove to be the anticlimax of the evening's festivities, compared to the horror-show provided by Ritchie's explosive ending.

Martin toiled on the cross, as Kilty did a sort of old man shuffle to the supersonic bass of some OG beats, and strobe lights. Cigarettes and hashish provided the smoke. They'd soundproofed the catacomb, so there was no concern about the decibels disturbing the neighbors.

Elaine was there too. One of the hangers-on, so to speak. She'd lost her psyche sometime after the ouija session. It was during the walk home with Michael. Something had hidden in her shadows shadow, and stolen it. Now she was just another nonplussed hanger-on at the altar boys sacrilegious misdeeds.

As they rolled by night, a nocturnal doppelganger had split off from the daylight version of Elaine. It made her feel terminally conflicted, guilty, and used up, depleting her of the life-force that powered her will to say no. She could discern between what was right and wrong—but didn't give a fuck anymore.

As for empathy, the only people who could identify

with what she was going through and confide in, were well past the point of no return. She'd swum past the mental warning buoys and been sucked into the riptide of degeneracy. The only way for her to survive was to go with it and deal with wherever she ended up on the other side. She couldn't repress this thing of supreme ickiness any longer.

It was a grey, slimy creature, with great big, black eyes—shiny but impenetrable, like marbles, and smiled at her with long, sharp, needle-like teeth. It whispered evil thoughts and had rotting fish breath. It tried to get her to do bad stuff—the kinds of things that made you go blind and grow hair on the palms of your hands. It lived by a subterranean stream of shit, inside everyone, and had risen from the sewer with the flood, drowning out everything else.

When she tried to explain what was going on inside her to her parents, they sent her to have a chat with Father Kilty, thinking the monster was a metaphor for their daughter's dreaded—budding sexuality, and thought a priest best suited to vanquish these ideas from her pretty little head. He told her to pray. She did. She still believed in God, it was an undeniable part of her conditioning, but the fight to hold on to this idea—to keep it alive within her was exhausting, and crazy-making, hence her surrender to the shadow within her shadow and her presence at the soul transference. The sullen, goth chick sitting in the corner, chain-smoking cigarettes.

The others were like the rabid audience at a satanic kiddie show, the ones who begged to be picked for one of the paedo host's audience participation segments, or get their birthday announced over the air, but never did.

'How does it feel Martin—this divine punishment?' Martin wasn't home at the moment. He could hear the same train barreling down the fissures of his brain as the one he'd succumbed to as a kid in the dentist's chair when he'd sucked up too much of the nitrous oxide and passed out. Kilty batted away one of the children who had been pestering him for his attention the whole night and continued.

'I almost envy you, your suffering. However, there will be plenty of time for that with my new body.' They led Mike to a lovely Carvelle table (donated by one of the parishioners for the church's annual silent auction, but had mysteriously disappeared the night before along with an electric carving knife), and made to lie down. He had the same look in his eyes as his former paramour, Elaine. A detached, far-away look. Shell-shocked. The one hundred-yard stare. He did not see things so much, as look right through them. Like the victim at a bombing, unscathed by the flying debris and body parts, but left deaf and dumb by the percussion of the blast. Martin was back for a second and managed to ventilate a question to Kilty.

'What happens to the old one—your body?' Kilty's pierced man-boobs jiggled, as he swayed back and forth, hypnotized by the snake charmer's music playing in his head, but snapped out of it to answer him.

'Nothing more than an empty vessel. Another compliant zombie to do my bidding. As to what that might be, maybe I'll have it grow a beard and work as a mall Santa. For the procurement of fresh lovelies. How's that sound?'

Gaap had entrenched himself in a vacant hemisphere in Kilty's brain. Lately, he'd stay put, until Kilty was engaged in something titillating; otherwise, this possession had become a burdensome chore, and he could hardly wait for the transmigration from Kilty's desecrated body to a newer smelling one; a lease rather than an outright purchase. Gaap didn't own anybody outright but could trade them in when he got bored and irritatingly spotted next years model that year. That was the problem with the whole possession thing, while it allowed him to feel some of the pleasures, and sweet suffering of humanity, it usually kept him bound to one being, obliged to them until his seal, a talisman created by the summoner, was disinterred, and then destroyed.

Fortunately for Gaap, though Kilty had forgotten where he'd put the sigil, he was killing two birds with one stone, affecting Gaap's transference, without binding him to Mike. There would be remnants of Kilty's psyche, but they would be the equivalent of EVP—ghostly voices on the periphery of human awareness.

Let's get this party started, Gaap thought, as Kilty doubled over from another pang of pain from cancer eating away at his guts.

The revelers began to settle and gather around the Saturday bingo and square dance callers stage. Kilty indicated to the de facto DJ, to cut the music. For the first time in the evening, the Hellmouth could be heard. It sounded like a combination of indigestion, and wind from a bloated stomach, after the inevitable overindulgence at a Thanksgiving feast, and the distant screeching of marauding banshees, flying up from the depths, to abscond with an offering. It had grown from a small crack in the concrete floor to a gaping chasm. The opening had jaws of great, dinosaur-sized teeth, set in disease-riddled gums, and belched a rank-smelling odor when it glowed and pulsated, and whispered foul sounding, barely discernible things. It was kept covered venerably, by a reliquary cover that one of the boys had built on the sly in woodworking class. No one dare be alone with the thing, especially girls, for fear the lash of a tongue would snatch them from the earth, and unlike Kilty—it preferred pussy.

He began the ritual by summoning, once again, his demon benefactor. The DJ had suggested some rousing intro-music, something along the lines of the stuff they played while boxers entered the ring, but they vetoed the idea for being too corny, and a buzzkill to the sinister vibe they were trying to create.

Kilty tried to pull the ceremonial dagger from its bejeweled scabbard, but it was stuck. It had been a long time since he'd last used it and was probably dull too.

Some of the kids snickered, and Elaine finally succeeded in generating a spark of sympathy for Martin, but quickly stifled herself to avoid the soul-crushing glare of her master. He was finally able to release the blade by having one of his assistants hold on to one end, while he braced his foot on the boy's face, and jerking spasmodically on the handle.

He tried to slice Martin's throat with a degree of ease and elegance, the way his priest had separated breast from bone, but ended up having to saw and carve at Martin's neck, forgetting how tough human skin is, and making a grotesque mess of the whole thing. His sacrifice was already gone, though, well away before his heart was ripped out—still fluttering involuntarily, and Martin shared his last gasp in tandem with the thrilled and grossed out kids. Hurled aboard the Nighthawk Express, and crammed into a packed subway carriage, just another anonymous commuter, jostled and pickpocketed by the other grotesqueries in search of currency, on a train bound for nowhere.

Aleister, looked out upon his beloved Loch-Ness, from a

spy-hole he'd torn in the wormhole. He felt a mix of exhilaration and terror as the wind ruffled his flesh, and bared his teeth. Fitting, as he'd have to marshal much psychic brawn before confronting the evil he had unleashed in Boleskine House after his last go-round with the Abramelin rite. Stupidly leaving them to their own wicked devices, after making the novitiates mistake, of failing to banish them back into the hellhole from whence they came.

The cavern, as the estate agent had called it, was considered a blight by the house's previous owners, but was the primary attraction for Aleister. He'd gotten the idea to traverse hell itself (a return to his origins and preview of his future destination if his detractors were to be believed), after he'd gained the superpowers promised to the magician, with the successful completion of the ritual.

One night while entertaining neighbors, he had to stomp on the thing's tongue, to stop it from slithering up the dress of one of the drunken dames.

He rewound the time of his arrival to the era just after Jimmy Page, of Led Zeppelin fame, had sold it to an anonymous buyer; the period the house sat empty before the new owner took possession. The manor had only just nearly burnt down, suffering damage to sixty percent of the structure. The result of a mysterious fire, and was now for sale once again. The hope was that some wealthy occult enthusiast as would come along and restore the house to its former glory.

The truth, and Aleister was well-versed in its mythology, was the house had a history of strange occurrences, long before he had ever set foot in the parish. The place was as old as they come, built in the thirteenth century as a church. According to local lore, the first conflagration occurred during a Sunday mass, after the hellhole had suddenly flared, and one of the roof beams had caught fire, killing all the worshippers in attendance.

The second significant supernatural event had been a mass resurrection of corpses in the graveyard, that had the pastor running around after them attempting to re-bury them in their proper plots. The house had been many things over its long history, including a hunting lodge, and a brief—failed incarnation as a hotel. He neither wished to bear witness to his life's greatest failure and watch himself stupidly leave without banishing the demons after he'd done or the guitarist's hackneyed attempts to finish what he'd started. He could only imagine the wimpy sounding, nasal inflected intonations, and the unfortunate mispronunciations of the complex, but sublime, magical lexicon that Abramelin had transcribed from the Gods themselves. He shuddered to think what further abominations the stoned aspirant had wrought upon his beloved temple.

He hovered a while over the rooftop as the axeman stowed the last of his luggage in the trunk of his sports car and tore off, kicking up gravel on to the artfully manicured garden path, then touched down at the doorstep.

Out of lifelong habit, he made the sign of the cross before stepping over the threshold and inhaled deeply of the centuries worth of scents that had seeped into the pores of the hand-hewn stone walls. There was frankincense from his days at the manor, a more recent Asian blend from the latest interloper, and another one he couldn't and wouldn't want to put a finger on. It was a sickening-sweet musk that went past the sensations in his nose and invaded the empty, dusty chamber that had been his stomach for the last eight decades or so.

As he continued down the corridor, he began to feel like the invitee to a party planned as a ruse for his ambush. He knew this feeling well as he'd been to many of these occasions before, both as the mastermind and unwitting victim. He was utterly bewildered for the first time since being led blindfolded into the Golden Dawn's ceremonial chamber, for his initiation into the first order. A mixture of fear and anticipation that felt like the butterflies with razor blade wings.

The interior, thus far, was surprisingly clean and tidy; 'Most likely the work of a scullery maid,' he said aloud, startling himself. He ran his finger along the crown molding to double check to see if the level of cleanliness was merely superficial, and clicked his fingers sharply to confirm that it was indeed, spotless. He expected it be stripped of its original charm and then re-filled with junk, or at least some wear and tear from the excesses typical of a rock star's life, but instead, it was tastefully outfitted with the now antique furniture of his era, and meticulously maintained. 'Like a church—just shut, after a poorly attended service,' he said.

However, it was what he came upon in the front room that made him swell with an appreciation for the apparent regard the young man had for Aleister's life and work. From the moment he again gently traversed the remnants of fine river sand, still scattered on the floor, and used during the ceremony, to detect the footprints of demons summoned. Then gazed up at his lovingly restored—divinely inspired, murals on the ceiling, and finally out at the breathtaking view through the crystal clear windows of the cantankerous loch, that he thought maybe the young whippersnapper had done it. Had achieved conversation and knowledge of his holy guardian angel. 'Little bugger beat me to it,' he said, smiling. If this was the case, for the first time in his long, notorious career, he didn't feel envy or enmity for another magician's accomplishment. Far from it. He felt genuine admiration and gladness that this ephemeral thing he'd spent a lifetime chasing, wasn't just another mythical metaphor, like medieval alchemy, but was now confirmed as being within the realm of possibility and at long last, his grasp.

With this enlightenment moment, he felt a tempered ecstasy from finally reaching the end of his journey along the path, that led to the place of his true will. The perfect fusion of desire and outcome; willing forth what was always meant to be. Every breath was a pleasure, free from the burden of a lifelong battle with asthma, and every exhalation was as calm and sure as the now glassy surface of the placid Loch. 'All time is now,' he sighed. Then, with the clunk of expensive luggage on the floor, and the fabled Nessie's, snake-like head, bursting forth from the agitated depths, his perfect peace was broken.

'Well. hello there.'
He turned around to see a smiling couple, in their late twenties. They were both bespectacled, true blondes, blue-eyed, with pearly white, chicklet teeth, and dressed in brand new, expensive-looking, outdoorsman gear. As American as blues music and apple pie. 'They can see me,' he said, loud enough for them to hear.

They looked at him queerly. 'You must be the letting agent.'

'No, no, former owner, back from the dead.'

They all chuckled—they unwittingly, at the truth. 'Jim kindly allowed me to reminisce. What brings you here?'

'Oh, morbid curiosity. Aleister Crowley, and spelunking.'

'Spelunking?' He thought the term had to be a

German activity requiring lederhosen, knee-slapping, and the cheering of beer steins.

'Yeah, there's a wild cave system that the house is built around. You must know of it. You owned the place.'

'Yes, of course.' They had no idea they were going to go spelunk into the very pit of hell.

'What do you think,' he said, pointing to the ceiling art.

'Primitive but effective. Evokes the primordial nature of evil, but is a bit mischievous as well—like the man himself.'

That was the best review he'd ever gotten. The stranger continued.

'He was not only a capable artist, but, as I'm sure you know, a great poet as well. He won the Nobel prize for literature. What else. Crowley was a philosopher, mountaineer, magician. I could go on...'

'Please do,' said Aleister, nodding his head in encouragement.

'I think it's whimsical,' she said.

They invited him to dinner and to join them for the few days he'd originally planned on. Afterall, they had large, empty rooms to spare, and would love the excuse to exploit the grand dining room with its vaulted ceilings and spectacular view of the Loch. He accepted the invitation without hesitation, and joined them after he'd retired to his former bedchamber, to plot out how he was going to go about the operation unencumbered by the presence of his unexpected guests. Strangely, he was looking for alternatives to slow torturous death and wanted to spare them the fate that awaited them, if they were to proceed with their expedition into the cave. He liked them. They were attractive, intelligent, and hadn't been petty or mean-spirited in their assessment of him, and in fact, had been quite effusive in their praise.

That evening, after the right wine—courtesy of Jim, as they called him, relaxed, stimulating discussion of all things under the sun—and even better weed, they decided to have a mosey around the manor and a gander at the hellhole.

They admired the intricate cover he'd had custom-made, and imported from a master artisan, specializing in the restoration of relics. It was decorated with an inlaid skull and crossbones, made from the most exquisite black pearl, and had the epitaph: Stratus

Descensus Averno carved in meticulous calligraphic lettering. Their enthusiasm seemed suddenly tempered though, by the thumping, and steam huffing and puffing from the box.

'You sure about this, honey,' she said, standing safely behind her partner.

'Just a build-up of gasses, muffin. Once we descend past the first pitch, it'll cool down. That's what the ski jackets are for.'

'I don't know. I think I'd rather go on that Nessie watching cruise,' she said. The hole started speak-wheezing to them, in a bronchial Latin patois, ending the blasphemous entreaty with a knowing cackle. The boyfriend's brave face and boyish eagerness died instantly.

'I have a far greater proposition for you.'

Barbie and Ken, slowly turned to look at Aleister's face, illuminated from below, like a jack-o-lantern, by the orange light that pulsed from cracks that spidered throughout the surface of the box, and they knew then his true identity. 'An adventure beyond your wildest dreams. Imagine possessing the power to travel back in time and rewrite history?'

They were instructed to pack lightly, and given Aleister's bank card for their trouble and expenses. She was already planning to be even more promiscuous, traveling back to her high school days, resuming her role as the notoriously frigid cheerleader, but this time taking up the star quarterback on his proposition of a foursome. He was for sure going to gather up the courage to not only go into a gay bar but not be such a stick in the mud and dance. They were instructed to pick up a friend of his first, before they embarked on any adventures, and drop him off wherever he wanted to go. With that, they were off, conveyed in supernatural style, into a vaster world of even more infinite possibilities.

When the moment finally came, after Kilty's rambling testimony to his greatness (the magical equivalent of an Allman Brothers guitar solo), Gaap, seized it. And with the awkward over-ebullience of a third-stringer, finally getting his shot in the dying minutes of a meaningless game—wrenched himself from Kilty's barren repression chamber—exploded out from his shadowless psyche, and manifested before the ecstatic assembly with every pyrotechnical trick in his arsenal. He'd left a little gift for any future brain pickers out there, in the corner, for having taken his sweet time.

Kilty's body folded in on itself to the stage floor, his head landing with the sharp smack of wet dough, his bones pulverized into a cancerous mash from Gaap's over-exuberant emergence. He attempted to raise his torso with wobbly arms and protest the desertion, but couldn't hold up his shattered remains, and collapsed down again, like a sand castle hit by a wave from an encroaching tide. His last words sounded like the static, crackling emergency transmission, from a broken CB radio. 'Help me.' Then the faint buzzing of a dying fly, 'Help me.'

The kids were ready to combust in anticipation for Gaap's next number, and he did not disappoint: flashing, stretching, spinning, and spiraling himself into a vortex at the center of a maelstrom-force whirlpool. He levitated toward Michael, hovering over his prostrate body when with one last prolonged inhalation; he was sucked wholly into the boy's flared nostrils. There was a reluctant smattering of applause, then Michael's body jerked and stiffened, the ligament, muscle, and bone, lengthening noisily, like rubber bands stretched to their limits, then plucked atonally, like the too-taught strings on a violin.

Once Michael's frame had attained the desired height, the skin commenced making noises like sticky-brittle plastic from the wrapping of a Christmas pudding, and Michael was hyper-aged before their eyes, to a handsome, healthy, and hench young man, in his mid-twenties. He rose from the slab slowly, like a laboratory monster, and with blazing eyes looked out upon the wary onlookers. He pointed to one of the frightened boys and sounding like their Michael—only older, and more vigorous, told him to fetch his vestments for mass.

They scooped up Kilty's jello-like remains and dumped them into the pit. The Michael they knew was still in there but trapped in a deep subconscious well, scratching and clawing at the slimy walls, trying desperately to escape, but in his weakened state, only getting so far before slipping back into the sludge. Gaap peered over the edge and waved at him then gave him the finger.

The service went off without a hitch, like a Siegfried show. The Tigers were tamed and dressed like altar boys. An announcement made by Gaap's and therefore Michael's favorite altar boy before their candlelit procession to the altar, of the peaceful passing of Father Kilty in the night, and the introduction of his replacement, Father Michael. Some feigned shock and sadness, and others openly rejoiced, giving flight to their glee in the overwrought singing of the hymns, one of them trilling like—drunk, Christina Aguilera. They all thought he looked vaguely familiar.

The parishioners liked this one. He struck them as being righteous, and straight as an arrow. Kind, and suitably affectionate, but tactfully restrained around the children. Some of the women thought him positively handsome; with those icy, fathomless blue eyes, and that devilish grin of his.

A gelatinous blob landed with a wobbly smack—right into Satan's lap. He'd resorted to doing what he always did when he'd packed it in—until some fool wanted to make a deal, or perhaps there'd be a resurgence in Satan worship amongst teens who wanted to give prospective girlfriends an excuse to cuddle up. He was curled up in Gaylord's lap, raptly listening to him read the Goetia, making him stop at the pictures and describe them to him in response to repeated, cutesy—What's that's?

He had redecorated his hellhole in grand, white trash fashion, utterly pillaged the Hammacher Schlemmer catalog for the latest man-cave gear and restlessly awaited the next delivery—just come, and for idle hands to present themselves.

Chapter 12

Jake parked the van as he always did on these types of missions, about a hundred yards from the intended target, and tucked between garages in a back alley. He handed them balaclavas and checked them for any identifying characteristics like scars or tattoos in conspicuous places. Tom passed with flying colors, but Tabitha required a body stocking.

It's scrunching my hair,' she whined, as Jake yanked the wooly over her face.

'They got CCTV all over the place. You can take it off when you get inside.'
Tom eased his on and had to pick an earlobe up off the oil-soaked gravel. Jake made sure the business part of

his his mullet was in place before carefully rolling on his, and they tiptoed out of the alley.

'I told you to wear flats,' he hissed, as she wobbled along in high heels.

'You also told me to be taller,' she said, giving him a sharp knock on his bony shoulder.

Tom thought the museum nondescript looking and wondered why buildings that were meant to be temples to one of the highest forms of human expression, always looked like utility buildings. They waited at the corner, inconspicuous as a trio disguised in balaclavas, in the dead of night, standing across the street from priceless works of art can be, and waited for cars to pass before crossing the street and hiding in an alcove in the wall.

'Concrete doesn't burn so well,' Jake said.

'It's just the one painting I need torching.'

'Unfortunately, we don't have the luxury of being too specific,' Jake said, tapping whatsername on the shoulder, indicating for her to remove the mask, and she revealing an even hotter, sweatier mess.

'How do I look?' she asked, as she foofed her hair and checked the rest of herself out in a narrow window.

'Fine,' Jake nodded and begged her off.

'You know the drill. Just make sure the door stays unlocked when you go inside, and when you hear the fire alarm let the security guard escort you to safety and catch the bus home.'

'You said you'd pay for a taxi,' she said, pouting her thin, trowelled-on lips.

'Bus—get your ass in gear.'

The whole thing was too stupidly-simple to succeed, but maybe that's why it was usually the idiots with their hare-brained schemes that pulled off the seemingly impossible, Tom thought, and repeated to Jake for some reassurance.

'It will, man, trust me; sex conquers all.'

Tom found that out for himself, back in Lonely Town. It could break down the resolve of the most stalwart men. Married, monogamous, even male menopause, couldn't stop sex's efficacy in corrupting morality and personal ethics. He thought he'd seen Jake grab the gas can. 'Look,' Jake said. ' I know there ain't no exhibition about everybody in heavy metal being queers and shit. What flamers you know wear leather and spikes? But I will use that one if I'm ever caught and have to convince a judge I'm batshit crazy, cause you had me at, well, fire, dude. I appreciate real art, too—I think, so we'll use my backup stuff instead, y' know, for a more discerning burn. Tom gave him the thumbs up and stifled himself from blurting out the Village People, like they were playing charades for money, and threw up his hands to say—'You're so right.'

Jake pulled a battered hip flask decorated with a German iron cross, from his breast pocket.

'I call it firewater—better accelerant than gasoline. 'The jerrycan is for mowing my folk's lawn later. See if we can't keep the carnage limited to your fav, and not deprive the rest of the art world their's.'

Tom savored every thought now. Every precious one of them. In hindsight, he didn't understand why people worked so hard to numb, slow down, or eradicate entirely—these now fascinating internal observations and monologues, either through legal or illicit means.

'This is a suicide mission, Jake. They're going to catch us and then string you up for this.'

'Naw, I gotta good feeling about this one. Like the Gods are looking out for us or something.'
Tom extended his stump to Jake, having left his hand in his pocket. They waited for the bait to work and lure the

rent-a-cop deeper into the exhibitions before removing their masks, and casually strolling in.

'Why is it people always whistle when they're trying to act casual? 'Tom whispered. 'Don't they know it's the universal sign for—that guy's definitely up to no good?'

Tom regretted that they couldn't linger longer, to succumb to Stendhal syndrome, and get dizzy with ecstasy at these dazzling emanations of life. He loved how they became even more expressionistic with the Doppler phenomena in full effect, from the frantic speed of their progress down the long corridors, like starved rats in search for aged cheese in a gilded maze.

Then they were there, and so were other thieves. *Nighthawks* seemed so infinitesimal compared to the giant Italian frescoes that surrounded it, yet had been his whole world for for God knows—how long.

The thieves were hired by the devil to help redecorate the hellhole, and were unfazed by their presence, nodding as they fled with the clear choice of epic, wall-sized masterpiece that would've been Tony Montana's choice.

Jake seemed thoroughly unimpressed by it. 'It's a painting of a restaurant, dude. Those were like

Mcdonalds back in the day. Whatever. Anyway, I gotta go to the head.'

'Are you fucking kidding me?' Tom knew Jake was going to do more than take a whizz, as he'd sheepishly admitted that masturbation was an integral part of his affliction.

'Just deposit this experience in your wank-bank and get on with it.'

He whipped out the flask and seemed suddenly entranced by the Pyro-God, as he sloppily doused the painting in the accelerant from his crotch region. Jake stopped and pulled out his phone to record the event for posterity, and lonely nights when his account at the bank of wank was overdrawn and needed an infusion of inspiration.

Tom swore he could see the little people in the diner scattering like stray sheep on the killing floor, as if they could see what was about to happen and tried to make their escape, tossing their newspapers, upturning coffee cups, and knocking on the toilet door to warn the others as they attempted to flee. Moreover, other things were lurking about that weren't in the original: Raven's shadow, cloaking the wolves as they barricaded the door, cleaving and howling at it to be let in. Tom also noticed for the first time that this place had an actual name: Phillies.

Jake pulled out his Zippo lighter, flicked the lid and did a guitar windmill as he lit it on a ripped patch of his denim jacket, and set that world ablaze. Tom's foot came off at the ankle, so he sat where he once stood and made himself as comfortable as possible on the floor, trying not to crumble before they'd done the job.

'What are you doing, man? Let's get the fuck out of here!'

'Come on, look at me Jake, I'm not going anywhere. Hey, thanks for the solid, bro. Grab a couple of shots before I'm dust, man.'

Just then they heard the stomping of their Jezebel, hightailing it toward them, with the equally jiggly security guard—hot on her heels. Only a tiny corner of the painting was left, and meanwhile back at the diner...

The atrophy of the building had suddenly ceased. A piece of the sidewalk was missing, but otherwise, Phillie's was still standing. Most of the regulars were still there except for Marilyn. She was the one the wolves had wanted as their bitch all along and had gotten the

Dahlia to lure her to them in exchange for the peace of Oblivion. Tom wondered if the Goddess had angels to take him away, as he felt his torso begin to cave.

Then from out of thin air, a window of infinite space opened up to them, and the constellations, thrown over them like a starry magician's sack. Jake and Tom were wrapped in a cloud of lush purple velvet, and conveyed in darkness, to what Tom thought would be oblivion; to sleep and never dream again.

Jake screamed like Rob Halford mid-coitus or chorus and pulled at the vehicle's seem, but then stopped, because they were there.

Outside the subway tunnel, with change already given for Tom's fiver, and a hot dog in his other hand. Jake snatched a newspaper from the stack in front of the cart. 'Aw, man, this is so like tomorrow—today, dude. I wanted to be whisked away, to post apocalyptic Chicago—chopping up zombies and shit.'

The headline of the day was: *Tragic Fire At Museum*, and the byline, a quote from the curator about the loss of priceless masterpieces, with *Nighthawks* mentioned last amongst them.

Tom double checked his cellphone and saw that it

was true. Another object was in his pocket. He withdrew a long gold, braided chain and a pocket watch that dangled from it. The fob was a bullet with a distinct dental pattern on the casing. The time was correct, and it was embossed with the big, bold initials, A.C. Were the teeth marks Aleister's or Fu's? Tom wondered.

Not that the loss of a day mattered. His wife would never suspect him capable of anything truly titillating, like infidelity, and work had transformed his cubicle to much-needed storage for all those stacks and stacks of numbers. He felt an ache in his restored belly and a tingle all over at the realization that it had all been real. That the most extraordinary chapter in his life was not an extended hallucination, like the time he'd fainted from a panic attack, when a movie followed you out of the theatre, or self-induced while daydreaming. However, it would seem so to others, if ever he was fool enough to recount the story of his epic adventure to his imagined cronies at the bar: the one where he was the hero for the first time in his life, and desired by a hot, goth chick, just like the techies in his preferred category of porn.

He remembered everything. It hit him like a boulder dropped from a tall tree and detonated, fizzing into his consciousness.

A young woman, smartly dressed in a military-ish looking uniform, approached them with a screwed-on smile.

'Would you like to take a personality test. It'll only take a few minutes?'

'No thanks, I just got one, Tom smiled back, gave her the thumbs up, and heard his teeth ting—just like a dish soap commercial.

'Get bent,' she said, then moved on, toward a guy in a fancy suit.

'What now?' Jake said, angling for a bite of Tom's hot dog.

'Gonna upgrade my phone and my wife. You know where I can get a pair of cowboy boots?' Tom asked, offering him the rest. 'You?'

'Fancy pants. Well, this time yesterday I was finishing rubbing one out in the staff head. I don't know, probably call in sick tomorrow. Get my shit together, and then maybe head out to LA.'

'Good man, that's the ticket, isn't it.'

They didn't exchange phone numbers and set themselves up for the inevitable guilt from failing to keep in touch. So with that, they shook hands and went their separate ways, both in new, uncharted directions. Tom wondered when the next church service was, and took the subway there, hugging the back wall while he waited for the sound of thunder, and Jake went to see if his van was still there.

'Later dude,' was all he said.

Tom wished he could give Aleister a shout. Go for a beer and shoot the shit. He'd never had a friend like him before—a real raconteur, man about town, type.

He was unaware that Aleister was only a subway stop away, gestating in the womb of his new earth-mother. The firstborn born to lower-middle-class parents residing in a modest, ranch-style house on the fringes of the suburbs-proper.

His new father was a staunch Irish Catholic, no-nonsense, hardworking sanitation worker, who'd always wanted a son to go on to do better things than him, to bring home the shekels. His wife was his frigid cheerleader—maybe virgin, high school sweetheart. The culmination of the great Abramelin rite had shrunken Aleister down to a spermatozoon, and from there deposited into one of his new father's hairy balls, then blasted out during the act of missionary coitus, and without any orgasmic pleasure of his own, battled his brethren for the honor of fertilizing his mother's egg.

He was an irascible fetus, always kicking up a fuss, but the doctor assured her that this was merely a portent of vigorous health, and vitality to come.

The dramatic conclusion to his life's work, the Abramelin rite, the transmission of ultimate enlightenment, was, a rebirth with his identity and faculties intact, but his wisdom trapped for now, in a child's slowly growing body.

They'd picked the name Bob—not Robert, like his new dad's dad before him. He was already plotting his overthrow of organized Christendom while basking in the comfort of his mother's warm waters. This time around he would retrieve the wormhole from Tom, travel back in time to enlist the great wizard, John Dee, and master his brand of Enochian magic. Together they would perform the old bait and switch, absconding with Jesus so that he might continue his ministry of love, and restore reincarnation as one of the cornerstone beliefs in their Gnostic branch of Christianity, and make it a philosophical belief system of the people—for the people.

However, this lofty ambition would have to wait. Bob would be forced to learn infinite patience—the one virtue that had eluded his last incarnation.

They proudly displayed baby Bob to Father Michael, who nearly recoiled and winced as he forced himself to give the obligatory kiss.

This babe knows of me—things that only the Satan is privy to, he thought. Gaap told him to order the execution of any male child two and under of every family in the parish like Herod before him but had yet to hold that kind of sway over his flock of seagulls. So like an enemy, he vowed to keep Bob close then closer still.

To my sublime wife and son Jaxon, to whom I owe my happiness and my very life. I'll love you both through the wormhole and back again. XXX

Printed in Great Britain
by Amazon

48934121R00129